CHERRIES, BERRIES AND A BODY

A CHOCOLATE CENTERED COZY MYSTERY

CINDY BELL

CONTENTS

ISBN: 9781080029693

CHAPTER 1

"Get back here, Peaches." Ally Sweet laughed as the orange cat bolted through the front door and headed straight towards the car. "You know you need your harness."

"I've got her." Charlotte Sweet scooped the cat up into her arms and looked back at her granddaughter. "She's pretty excited about this outing I see."

"I think she's just jealous of all the places we've been taking Arnold lately." Ally took her cat from her grandmother and cuddled her against the curve of her cheek. "Don't worry, sweetie, you're going to get your adventure today." She stroked her fur, then eased on her harness. "I think it's better if she has her new harness on today. She doesn't know Geraltin very well.

She likes to take off any opportunity she gets, and she might get lost if she takes off on her own there."

"I think the harness is a wise choice. As for this piggie, we're just going to have to hold on to the leash tight." Charlotte reached down and patted the top of Arnold's head. "All of the delicious smells are going to drive him wild."

"Very true. Look, he's already sniffing." Ally laughed as Arnold dug his snout into the dirt beside the car. "What did you find, Arnold?"

Arnold looked up at her with dirt-covered nostrils. One sharp snort sent the dirt flying through the air and shook the pig's body from his tail to the top of his head.

"See, Arnold." Charlotte clucked her tongue. "Being too curious can get you into trouble."

"Aw, he can't help it." Ally grinned as she watched Arnold step up into the backseat of the car. "It's just his nature."

"I thought curiosity was a cat's thing?" Charlotte settled into the driver's seat.

"Oh, this one is plenty curious, too." Ally scratched beneath Peaches' chin as she sat down in the passenger seat. "The two of them might just get us into a little bit of trouble today."

"I hope not. Bill and Starla's farm is a special place for me. Do you remember going there when you were little?" Charlotte flashed a smile in Ally's direction as she started the car.

"I vaguely remember fruit trees and the most delicious berries I ever tasted." Ally closed her eyes as she recalled the taste on the tip of her tongue. "It's amazing the things that stick out in your memory."

"Yes, it is." Charlotte sighed softly as she steered the car on to the main road. "I can still remember my first taste of a strawberry. I was a bit older than you are. Fruit was hard to come by when I was young, well certain kinds of fruit. The strawberry was a real treat. My father brought them home and we got to taste just one each. To this day, I've yet to taste anything sweeter."

"Not even your chocolates?" Ally looked over at her with an arched eyebrow. "I'd say they're pretty sweet."

"Yes, they are. But that strawberry, it was perfectly ripe, sweet with just a hint of tartness, and it melted on my tongue." Charlotte smiled as she turned on to the highway that would lead them to Geraltin, a much larger town, a couple of towns

3

over. "It's a different kind of sweet than sugar creates. It's natural, pure."

"That's why it's absolutely perfect for our candies." Ally rested her head back against the car seat and gazed out the window as they passed a few farms. "I'm so glad that we use Bill and Starla's fruit in our candies and that we are going to be increasing our range of fruit candies. Hopefully, it will help their farm, and I know that people love the combination of fruit and chocolate and will be happy that we will have more variety."

"Me too. It's exciting that we can use fruit directly from a nearby farm. I think increasing our range of chocolates using the fruit that has been dried or candied by us will be great. We should also look at adding more chocolate flavors with liquid fruit centers. Using real fruit and no artificial flavorings, feels more authentic and gives the candy a fuller taste. Also, I can't wait to try her jams and use them in our recipes." Charlotte took an exit off the highway. "Not far now, just about fifteen minutes. Hopefully, Arnold won't get too restless back there."

"Oh, I don't think we have to worry about that." Ally glanced over her shoulder at the backseat just as Arnold emitted a loud snore. The pig was sprawled out across his blanket, quite content to nap.

"Oh boy, that means he's storing up his energy." Charlotte laughed.

As they neared the farm, Ally glanced over at her grandmother.

"I really hope this works out. I think it will be a great opportunity for the shop."

"Me too. Since so many of our customers love natural and organic everything, offering locally sourced, organic jams in our baked chocolate creations will be a big hit." Charlotte turned down the long road that led to the farm. "I'm so excited to see what Starla came up with."

Once they'd parked, all four walked towards the large barn that was diagonal to the house that the farm owners lived in. Chickens scattered across the space between the two structures, and a stray goat wandered curiously in Arnold's direction.

"Hi there!" A woman stepped out of the open barn door and waved to them. She was thin and tall, about six feet with long, white hair, and a bright smile.

"Hi Starla!" Charlotte walked towards her, her own smile just as bright. The two greeted each other with a warm hug.

As Ally stepped towards them, she offered her hand to Starla.

"It's nice to see you, Starla."

"You too." Starla gave her hand a firm shake. "I'm so glad that you both could come out today. Thank you for coming a bit later, I am running late this morning." She brushed a white curl behind her ear and smiled as Arnold sniffed at her shoe. "I just knew that Arnold would love it here, and Peaches seems to be fitting in just fine with the barn cats." She glanced over at Peaches whose nose poked right up to the nose of another cat.

"Yes, she is." Ally eyed Peaches for a moment to be sure that the two cats wouldn't break out into a fight. However, a light swish of Peaches' tail indicated she was content with the introduction.

"I'm so excited for you to try these. I just know that you're going to love them." Starla stepped aside to reveal a small tray of jams in small containers.

"I'm excited, too." Charlotte's eyes flashed as she stared at the jams. "I've been hearing so much about them. Just about every one of your customers that comes into our shop is raving about these new jams."

"They are absolutely delicious. Go on, try a few."

Starla pointed to one specifically. "The apple berry cherry is my favorite."

"Sounds amazing." Ally helped herself to a small spoon and tasted the jam. As the jam melted on her tongue, she closed her eyes and sighed. "So good."

Charlotte offered a quiet moan as she tasted the jam as well. "Starla, you have outdone yourself. These might be the best jams I've ever tasted."

"I'm glad you like them, but I can't take credit for them. I'm not the one who makes the jams." Starla smiled.

"You're not?" Ally's eyes widened. "But everyone has said the new jams are from Bill and Starla's farm."

"Oh, they are. But I'm not the creator. One of my employees is. Her name is Elisa, and she is the one who has been making them. She's such a young girl, only about your age, Ally, and she has only been here for a few months, but she really has a natural talent with the fruit." Starla nodded.

"Can we buy some?" Charlotte met Starla's eyes. "We are definitely interested in getting some of the jams and using them in cakes and some other baked treats."

"I thought you might be." Starla winked at her. "Yes, Elisa is down at the shed in the orchard right now, you can arrange to buy some from her there if you want. I know she is very low on stock, but she can sort that out with you. I'll get someone to put the fruit you ordered in your trunk while you're out at the shed."

"Thanks." Charlotte smiled.

"I'll have Bobby give you a ride down on one of the carts. Arnold and Peaches can stay here in the barn if you'd prefer."

"That would be great, thanks." Ally nodded as she watched Peaches chase after one of the barn cats. Arnold was hot on the trail of another cat, with his snout snorting along the dirt.

"Bill is already out in the fields, but he said to say hello and he'll try and catch up with you before you leave." Starla looked at Charlotte. Charlotte had known Starla's husband, Bill, for most of her life. He was a quiet man and had a sweet tooth, which meant he would pop in to Charlotte's Chocolate Heaven to get some chocolates when he was in Blue River, which wasn't very often because he worked such long hours.

"That would be great." Charlotte smiled. "I haven't seen him in a while. These are for the two of you. I know they're your favorites." She handed her a box of chocolates.

8

"Thank you." Starla smiled. "How much do I owe you?"

"Nothing, of course." Charlotte shook her head. "It's a gift for having us out here."

"Thank you," Starla repeated.

"We'll see you soon, Starla." Charlotte gave a quick wave.

Ally stepped outside into the sunlight. As she glanced around, she heard the roar of an engine headed in her direction. She turned in the direction of the sound and spotted a golf cart as it barreled straight towards her. She had never seen a golf cart go that fast before, and guessed that some parts had been replaced in it. She stepped back as the cart drew closer. However, it seemed to her that the cart shifted in her direction at the same time. Was he trying to hit her?

"Hey!" Ally gasped as the cart squealed to a stop right in front of her. "Watch it!"

"Sorry about that, sometimes she gets away from me." He gave the steering wheel a sharp smack. "I'm Bobby. I'm here to take you out to the orchard."

"Okay." Ally regarded him hesitantly. Did she really want to get into the cart with him?

"Ready?" Charlotte stepped outside with a smile. "Bobby? I'm Charlotte and this is Ally." She offered him her hand. "Thanks for taking us out there."

"Anytime." Bobby gave her hand a quick shake. "Climb on, don't be shy." He revved the engine and grinned.

"Mee-Maw, maybe we should just walk, it's a nice day." Ally frowned as she eyed Bobby.

"Nonsense, it's too hot for that. These old legs need a rest." Charlotte winked as she climbed up into the cart.

"Yeah right, those legs will never be old." Ally climbed in beside her. "I'm going to have to start doing yoga, so I can keep up with you."

As the cart lurched forward, Ally found it impossible to speak. She was too busy gritting her teeth against the bumps and swerves that Bobby put them through. Ally grabbed on to the frame of the golf cart to keep from sliding into her grandmother, and noticed that her grandmother did the same. Luckily, the ride was fairly fast thanks to Bobby's lead foot. As the cart screeched to a stop in front of a small shed, she breathed a sigh of relief.

"Here we are, ladies." Bobby flashed them a grin. "Safe and sound."

Ally climbed out, then turned back to make sure that her grandmother made it out okay.

"Thanks for the ride, Bobby." Ally glanced at her grandmother with wide eyes.

"Yes, thanks." Charlotte held back a laugh as she leaned a hand on Ally's shoulder to steady herself.

"Oh, can you give this to Elisa please? With the heat, Starla likes to make sure that all of the staff remain hydrated." Bobby held out a large bottle of water. "It's hard to keep things cold this far out."

"Sure." Ally smiled and took the bottle.

Bobby waved to them both, then took off across the farm.

"That was worse than any roller coaster ride I've ever been on." Charlotte broke out with the laughter she had been holding back. "Do you think he hit every bump on purpose?"

"I think he did." Ally grinned as she stared after the cart.

"He has to know this property well enough to know his way around the bumps. He sure didn't seem to mind them." Charlotte smoothed down her blouse and glanced in the direction of the shed in front of them.

"Ugh, I think we're better off walking back." Ally shook her head.

"I don't know, that's a long walk." Charlotte

11

gazed out across the expansive farm. "Bill and Starla have done very well for themselves."

"Yes, they have." Ally reached up and knocked lightly on the door of the shed. "This must be where Elisa is."

"It is." A warm voice greeted them as the door began to slide open. Beyond it was a woman with bright brown eyes, and a wide smile. "Charlotte and Ally, right?"

"That's us." Ally thrust out her hand to her. "I'm so pleased to meet the woman who creates such delicious concoctions."

"Ah, it's good stuff, isn't it?" Elisa grinned as she shook her hand. "I'm happy to meet the two of you as well. I've heard so much about both of you from some of my customers. I'm glad to finally meet you."

"This is from Bobby." Ally held out the bottle of water.

"Thank you." Elisa smiled as she took it.

"We also brought you something." Charlotte handed her a small box of assorted chocolates. "So, you can get a taste of the kind of chocolates we make."

"Oh yes, I hoped you might bring me some." Elisa waved them inside the shed. "It's a tight space, I know, but it's mine. Starla was kind enough to let me use it for sorting out the fruit for the jams and storing the empty jars and labels. I have a small kitchen set up with a couple of burners and a refrigerator at the back of the house."

"Starla said you hadn't been here very long." Ally looked around the shed. There were several shelves lined with glass mason jars. "It looks like you're all organized here."

"Thanks, but to be honest, I've already outgrown it here. I store the finished products at the house. Luckily, the jams have been flying out the door, so storage hasn't been too much of an issue, but I want to have proper facilities. I'm hoping that I can make enough from this next round of products to rent myself a small space in town." Elisa set the box of chocolates down on one of the shelves and turned to face the two women. "At least I'll have a place to store the jams."

"Well, maybe we can help you with that." Charlotte smiled as she met the woman's eyes.

"Really?" Elisa wiped her hands on the towel attached to her belt and looked between both them.

"We had considered just asking to buy some of your jams to use in our products on a regular basis, but then we thought of something better." Ally smiled as she looked over at her grandmother.

"We would like to create a partnership with you. We would like to stock your jams and other products in our shop for sale. In return we would like to be able to sell some of our fruit chocolates and baked goods here on the farm." Charlotte smiled at Elisa. "What do you think?"

"I think it sounds like a fantastic offer." Elisa shook her head as her eyes widened. "I've been wanting to expand, and to be able to sell my jams in Blue River would be a wonderful opportunity for me. But it isn't my business. I would need to check with Starla if it's okay and work out pricing with her."

"Of course, we can work all of that out." Charlotte shrugged. "I love to see a business being started from the ground up. My chocolate shop started in my kitchen, as Christmas gifts for my neighbors. If I hadn't given it a chance to grow, I would never have gotten to where I am today."

"It sounds like a great opportunity, and I'm sure we would work well together." Elisa looked over at Charlotte. "Can I take some time to think about it and talk to Starla?"

"Absolutely." Charlotte nodded and flashed her a

smile. "And please feel free to contact us if you have any questions, or you want to discuss it."

"Thank you both." Elisa took Charlotte's hand and gave it a firm shake. "I'm sure we can work something out together."

"We would like to get two jars of jam, please." Ally smiled. "One apple berry cherry and one blueberry."

"Oh, I'm sorry. I'm all sold out." Elisa frowned. "But I am making a fresh batch tomorrow. I can drop them off at the chocolate shop later in the week, and that way I can have a look at the shop."

"Great." Charlotte winked at her. "I'm looking forward to giving you a tour. Now, we'll let you get back to work."

"Wait." Elisa picked up a jar of raspberry jam. "This is a fresh batch which I'm already almost sold out of, please take it as a gift. You can try it out and see how you like it."

"Thank you." Charlotte smiled.

"It was nice meeting you, Elisa." Ally waved to her, then followed her grandmother out of the shed.

CHAPTER 2

A sharp beep alerted Charlotte and Ally to the presence of Bobby, and his golf cart.

"Starla sent me to pick you up." He smiled.

Ally glanced at her grandmother. "It's still too hot to walk right?"

"Aw stop." Bobby blushed. "I'm a great driver you know."

"Yes you are, Bobby." Charlotte patted his arm. "And we are very grateful for the ride." She met Ally's eyes. "The sooner we get back to the shop the sooner we can start experimenting. Right?" She winked at her.

"Right." Ally reluctantly climbed into the golf cart. Her grandmother stepped in beside her.

Ally barely had time to get settled when Bobby

gunned the engine. She braced herself against the frame and tried to keep her stomach calm as they tore over the bumpy path back towards the barn.

"I can't wait to try out some of this in my white chocolate raspberry cake when we get to the shop." Charlotte clutched the jam jar tightly, as Bobby drove right over yet another bump.

"If it makes it that far." Ally winced and grabbed on to the side of the cart, as it lurched.

"Oh, it will." Charlotte wrapped her arms around the jar.

When they reached the barn, Ally stepped out of the cart with relief. As she steadied herself, she looked back at Bobby.

"Do you need a license to drive this thing?"

"The way I do, sure." Bobby grinned at her with a gleam in his eyes that made her certain he'd given them a rough ride on purpose. As he tore off down the path she was tempted to shout after him. When she turned towards the barn, she was even more tempted to tell Starla exactly how she felt about Bobby. But before she could reach the barn door, Starla came running out.

"Charlotte! Ally! I'm so sorry!"

"It's all right." Ally managed a smile. "I'm sure he was just trying to be funny."

"What?" Starla's eyes widened. "I don't know what you mean. But I have to tell you, Peaches and Arnold, they're gone!"

"Gone?" Charlotte took a few steps towards the barn. "What do you mean gone?" She stuck her head inside the barn and called out for Arnold. "He's probably just hiding."

"No, he's not. I've looked everywhere." Starla wrung her hands as she turned her attention to Ally. "One second they were there, and the next I couldn't find them anywhere. I don't understand it. Do they often run off together?"

Charlotte and Ally exchanged a long look as their minds filled with the numerous times Peaches and Arnold had worked together to get themselves into trouble.

"It does happen." Ally frowned. "But that's always back home. They don't know the area here. We'd better look for them."

"I can get Bobby on the radio!" Starla reached for the radio on her belt.

"No please." Charlotte held up one hand. "We can just walk. Arnold probably left some tracks we can follow. It's all right, Starla. It's not your fault. Those two are just so mischievous." She rolled her eyes and smiled. "Don't worry, we'll find them."

"I can help you look." Starla pulled the barn door shut behind her. "Let's go, before they get too far."

"Thanks." Ally swept her gaze across the farm. She tried to be as calm as her grandmother appeared to be, but underneath she was worried. Peaches and Arnold didn't usually take off very far unless they had a good reason, which meant they probably went wherever they went quite quickly. The thought of the two of them lost on such a vast farm made her head swim with anxiety. "Peaches!" She began to scour the ground for any sign of tracks. However, with so many animals on the farm, the dirt was littered with tiny prints. They all blurred together to make following them impossible.

"This isn't going to work." Charlotte frowned as she led the way down a path between two fields. "I think we should split up. We have no way of knowing which way they went."

"Wait." Ally glanced around the farm again. "They wouldn't have just wandered off. If they found their way out of the barn, they had a reason. There's nothing on this farm that I can see that would really draw their attention that much. The only thing familiar to them here, is us."

"Our scents." Charlotte nodded as her eyes

widened. "You're right, Ally. If they're lost, they are probably trying to find their way back to us."

"They might have been trying to find us in the first place." Ally glanced over her shoulder at the barn again. "We should retrace our path to the shed. Maybe they're with Elisa right now."

"I'll check. She has a radio in the shed." Starla pulled the radio off her belt. She twisted the button on the top, and loud static blared through the speaker. She pressed down the button on the side of the radio and held it. "Elisa, are you there? Answer, please." She released the button and waited.

Ally stared at the radio. Surely, Elisa would answer that she was there, and so were Peaches and Arnold. Then all of this would turn out to be nothing more than an inconvenience.

Starla glanced at the radio, then pressed the button on the side down again.

"Elisa, answer please. We have a missing pig and cat." She released the button. "I'm sure she's just busy with something."

"Let's just get going." Charlotte began to walk again. "I'm sure that we'll find them waiting there for us, if not along the way."

"Right behind you." Ally fell into step behind her grandmother.

Starla tucked the radio back into its holster and matched her pace with theirs.

"You know, they might have gone towards the pond. It's warm out today, maybe they wanted a drink?" Starla gestured across one of the fields. "There's a short cut to it this way."

"We can check there if they're not at the shed." Charlotte wiped some sweat away from her forehead. She found herself actually wishing to be back in Bobby's cart. But she didn't want to miss any sign that the animals might have left behind. "Ally, look!" She crouched down and pointed to a dug-up area at the side of the trail. "I'd know that snout print anywhere. Arnold has been here!"

"And my guess is that Peaches wasn't far behind." Ally scanned the surrounding fields. "But I don't see any sign of them now. At least we know that we're going in the right direction. Let's hurry."

"Arnold!" Charlotte called out as she continued down the path at a quicker pace. "Arnold, get back here!"

"There's the shed." Ally sighed with relief as she spotted it in the distance. Her back was drenched in sweat. The hot sun continued to beat down on her. "I still don't see them, though."

"Like I said, I think the pond is a good place to

check. Why don't I head that way? I'll let Bill know what's happening so he can keep an eye out as well." Starla looked between both of them. "Have Elisa call me on the radio if you find them at the shed."

"Okay." Charlotte offered her a smile. "Thanks for all of your help, Starla."

"Absolutely. I just hope we find them fast. They shouldn't be out in this heat for too long." Starla hurried off across the field in the direction of the pond.

Ally and Charlotte approached the shed quickly.

"I'm sure they're here." Ally's heart pounded as she looked around the outside of the shed. She noticed a few paw prints, but she couldn't be sure that they belonged to Peaches, since there were other cats on the farm. Still, she hoped they belonged to her.

"Elisa?" Charlotte knocked lightly on the door of the shed. "Are you in there?"

A loud snort drew both of their attention.

"Arnold!" Ally darted around the side of the shed. "He's back here, Mee-Maw!" She crouched down and opened her arms to the pig. Arnold rushed towards her, snorting and squeaking at the same time. His snout was caked in mud. "It's all right, buddy, we found you."

"Oh Arnold, there you are." Charlotte shook her head and smiled. "You gave us a bit of a scare. But where is Peaches?"

"I'm not sure." Ally frowned as she looked past the pig towards the end of the shed. "I bet she isn't far, though."

"You go look around for her. I'll keep Arnold with me." Charlotte straightened up and walked around the side of the shed.

As Ally rounded the corner, she spotted a familiar tail flicking through the air.

"Peaches! I've got her, Mee-Maw!"

"Oh good!" Charlotte rounded the corner with Arnold by her side. When she spotted the cat, she smiled. "I guess we've got our adventurers."

"Peaches, you naughty cat." Ally reached down to pick her up as Peaches swung her head around. Her normally orange face was coated with a dark red. "Peaches!" Ally took a step back. The sight of the cat was startling. "What have you gotten into?" She edged forward, towards the cat.

Peaches had turned her attention back to the shed, more specifically the dirt right at the side of it. She dug her paws through it. Ally noticed that Peaches' paws were also covered in something red and sticky. "Ugh, what is that? Mee-Maw, what do you think?"

"Ally, get her." Charlotte frowned as she watched the cat dig at the dirt. "Something isn't right here."

Ally scooped Peaches up into her arms. Peaches squirmed in an attempt to get down. As soon as she brought the cat close to her face, she smelled how sweet the sticky, red substance was.

"I think it's strawberry jam." Ally looked past the cat, towards the shed, and watched as a dark red puddle oozed out from under the side of it. "Elisa must have spilled something."

"Or these two found a way in and made a mess." Charlotte winced at the thought. "We'd better check. We're going to have to pay for any damage they might have done."

"You're right." Ally shook her head at her cat, who had begun to purr. "Don't you even think about nuzzling me with that dirty mug. You're getting a bath as soon as we get home."

Peaches squirmed even more at the word 'bath'. Ally held her tight as she walked around the side of the shed, back to the front. She pushed the door open and peered inside. "Oh no!" She stared at the shelves where there had been jars lined up. Now they were scattered all over the floor. "What did you two do?" She glanced from Peaches to Arnold.

"How did they even get in there with the door closed?" Charlotte sighed. "I guess it doesn't matter. We'd better find something to clean this up with."

Charlotte stepped inside the shed. As she did, Arnold began to squeal. The pig's cries almost drowned out Charlotte's gasp.

"Ally! Call for help!" Charlotte rushed towards the crumpled body in the corner of the shed. It only took a moment for her to see that it was Elisa. She checked for a pulse but found none. As she gazed at the young woman, she realized that it was far too late, she was already gone.

CHAPTER 3

*a*lly's heart raced as she called for help. She gave the location of the farm, and the location of the shed as best she could. A radio came to life on Elisa's hip.

"Elisa, have you spoken with Ally and Charlotte? Did you find the animals?"

Ally's stomach twisted with dread as she recognized Starla's voice.

"I should answer her." Charlotte reached for the radio on Elisa's hip.

"No, Mee-Maw. Don't." Ally gestured for her to come closer. "We shouldn't touch anything more than we have. The police are going to need to find out exactly what happened here."

"You're right. This was no accident." Charlotte

backed away from Elisa's body and stepped out of the shed beside Ally. As Ally continued to relay what information she could over the phone, Charlotte kept Peaches and Arnold close to her. "Did you two know that something was going on here? Is that why you broke out of the barn?" Charlotte frowned as she stroked her hand across the top of Arnold's head.

As Ally recalled the scene inside the shed, she considered how Elisa might have died. She did have several small cuts, was she stabbed? She ended the call and turned back towards the shed. She wished she could roll back time just long enough not to leave Elisa alone.

"Who could have done this?" Ally sighed as she surveyed the ground outside of the shed. The ground around the door was so scuffed that there wasn't any way to tell whose footprints belonged to who. As she backed away from the door a few feet, the ground was torn up by the tracks of Bobby's golf cart. She doubted that the police would be able to get much evidence from the ground. She looked back up at the door itself. It hadn't been locked when they arrived, the first time or the second time. Elisa's killer could have easily just walked in on her.

The door didn't have much of a handle, would there be fingerprints?

"I don't even know how this could happen. We were just here!" Charlotte walked over to Ally.

"I know." Ally pressed her hand against her stomach. "I keep thinking that if we had just stayed a little longer, maybe we could have protected her." She bit into her bottom lip. Then a chilling thought swept through her mind. "Mee-Maw, what if her killer was here when we were? Maybe the person who did this was hiding nearby and waited until we left to strike?" She looked around for any good places to hide in the surrounding area.

"It's possible." Charlotte followed her gaze. "But I don't know where they would have hidden. The fields are so wide open here."

"There." Ally pointed towards the orchard where a few trees were clustered close together. "That might give enough cover to hide a person."

"It could." Charlotte nodded, then shot a sideways look at Ally. "Let's have a look."

Ally nodded as she met her grandmother's eyes. If there was one thing neither of them could walk away from, it was a mystery that needed to be solved.

Arnold and Peaches walked right beside them as they headed for the trees. Ally was careful to watch for any evidence on the ground as they walked. Perhaps there would be a blood trail, or a deep scuff mark from a shoe. But all she saw was grass and soil.

"I'll look on this side, you take the other side." Charlotte gave the instruction with confidence in her voice. She tended to have a take-charge attitude in crisis situations. Ally was grateful for it, as her head still spun with the memory of finding Elisa. She walked around behind the trees and began to look through the grass that surrounded them. She stopped as she noticed a pile of cherry pits and stalks on the ground.

"Mee-Maw! I think I found something!" Ally took a step back, determined not to contaminate what could be evidence.

"What is it?" Charlotte peered over her shoulder.

"Some cherry pits. Maybe someone waited here and ate some while we were inside the shed." Ally frowned as she looked through the branches of the trees in the direction of the shed. "It gives a clear view right into the shed through the window. Can you see it?"

"Yes, I can." Charlotte narrowed her eyes. "We

have to make sure that we show this to the police. We'd better get out of this area just in case there is any other evidence here for them to find."

"You're right." Ally scooped up Peaches and carried her as they walked back up to the shed. As they reached it, a police car rolled up the narrow path towards them.

After the police made their initial assessment of the situation, one officer pulled Charlotte aside, and another pulled Ally aside.

"Can you tell me what happened here?" The younger officer met Ally's eyes. "Did you see or hear anything?"

"No, we found her when we got here." Ally frowned. "We just had a meeting with her not long ago. Then my cat and my grandmother's pig escaped, and we went looking for them. We found them here."

"Your cat and your grandmother's pig discovered the murder?" The officer pursed his lips.

"That's what happened, Officer. That's all I can tell you." Ally frowned, then glanced over her shoulder at the patch of trees. "We do think we might have found some evidence of someone watching the shed. There are some cherry pits over there behind those trees. Maybe the killer was eating cherries and watching. He or she might have waited for Elisa to be alone."

"It seems like you have this all figured out." The officer tucked his pen behind his ear, then crossed his arms. "Maybe you know a bit more than you're saying?"

"No, sir." Ally looked back at him. "I can understand why you may feel the need to suspect me, but I had nothing to do with this, and neither did my grandmother. You'll be wasting your time if you think we did."

"I'll keep that in mind." The officer pulled his pen from behind his ear and made a note on his notepad.

"Please, you can think what you want about me, but make sure you check out those cherry pits, okay?" Ally tried to meet his eyes, but he refused to look at her.

"Barker, I'm done with this one." He called out to the older officer.

Charlotte shot a sharp look in the direction of the officer who described Ally as 'this one'. She didn't like his tone one bit. As she turned her attention back to the officer who questioned her, she did her best to sound patient.

"Officer Barker, I appreciate that you need to question me but if you just ask Starla, one of the owners of the farm, she will tell you that she was just with us searching for our pets. My granddaughter and I had nothing to do with what happened to Elisa." Charlotte settled her gaze on him.

"We'll do a walkthrough of the crime scene, but the two of you need to stay put. Okay?" Officer Barker adjusted the hat on his head.

"Yes, sir." Charlotte did her best to sound polite.

Before either officer could begin their search, a golf cart came careening towards them.

"Slow down!" Officer Barker shouted as he stepped out in front of Charlotte. "You stop that vehicle right now!"

Bobby swung the cart around and continued towards the shed. Ally spotted Starla in the passenger seat.

"Stop!" The younger officer drew his weapon and aimed it at the cart as it sped right towards him.

"Bobby, hit the brakes!" Ally shouted at him as he barreled towards them.

The brakes squealed as Bobby stepped on the

pedal at the last minute. The cart spun up some dirt, then rocked, and finally stopped, a few feet away from the officers.

"What's going on here?" Starla stepped out of the cart and looked between Charlotte, Ally, and the pair of police officers that stood before them. "I see you found your animals, was there really a need to get the police involved?"

"Starla." Charlotte touched the woman's shoulder gently. "I'm afraid something terrible has happened."

"Terrible?" Starla looked from Charlotte, to the two officers, then back again. "What could be so terrible?"

"We found Peaches and Arnold, but we also found Elisa. I'm sorry to tell you this, but she's passed away. It looks like she's been killed." Charlotte gazed into the woman's eyes.

"What?" Starla stumbled back a few steps. "What are you talking about? Elisa?" She looked towards the shed. "Elisa! Is this some kind of game?" She looked wildly back at the officers.

"No ma'am, I'm sorry." The younger officer moved to her side and grasped her by the elbow to steady her. "I know it must be a shock. But we have confirmed that she has passed away. I'm very sorry for your loss."

"My loss," Starla mumbled, then looked up at the shed again. "How could this happen?"

"As you know, we had just seen her, not long before." Charlotte clutched Ally's hand and shivered. "When we got here, there was no response inside. We thought that we would check inside. That's when we found her."

"Oh no, oh dear, oh no." Starla's breathing became ragged. "What am I going to do?"

"There's nothing for you to do right at this moment." The officer led her towards his police car. "Other than to sit down and take a few deep breaths."

"Wait!" Starla pulled back from the officer and spun on her heel. "Bobby! We have a killer loose on the farm! Make sure everyone knows, make sure everyone is safe!"

"Yes Starla." Bobby pulled out his radio and leaned back against the side of the cart. As he began to bark into the radio, the officer guided Starla to the car once more.

"Let's get you sitting down. Sometimes a shock like this can make you light-headed or dizzy. I don't

want to see you get hurt." The officer pulled open
the back door of the car.

"No!" Starla shrieked and tugged away from
him, which caused her to barrel right into Charlotte.
"No, you'll never get me inside of that car! I didn't
do anything wrong!"

"Ma'am, calm down, you're not under arrest."
The officer held up his hands in surrender. "I just
want to make sure that you're okay."

"Sure, you do." Starla glared at him, then leaned
into Charlotte's arms. "Please, Charlotte, I'm not
feeling very well."

"Why don't you sit down in the cart?" Charlotte
looked towards Bobby. "Bobby, can you help us
here?"

"Sure." Bobby tucked the radio back into the
holster on his hip, then slipped his arm around
Starla's waist. As he eased her into the cart, she
began to cry.

"Oh Elisa, how did this happen?" Starla wiped
at her eyes. "She was such a sweet girl. Why would
anyone ever do this to her?"

"That's what we intend to find out." The officer
rested his hands on his hips.

They all turned in the direction of a tractor
coming towards them.

CHAPTER 4

The tractor stopped beside the police car and Bill climbed down off it. He was a tall, intimidating figure, and besides the love he openly displayed for his wife, he never showed any emotion. He had weathered skin and wore a baseball cap over his balding, gray hair. His white shirt and jeans were covered in mud. Despite his age, he ran with ease over to Starla.

"What's happened?" Bill took his wife into his outstretched arms.

"It's Elisa." Starla's voice shook.

"Elisa?" Bill pushed her back and looked into her eyes. When she didn't reply, he looked towards the officer.

"I'm afraid, she's deceased." The younger officer's voice softened. "I am sorry for your loss, sir."

"Clyde." Bill guided his wife back into the seat in the golf cart. "What happened?"

"She's in the shed, sir. We don't know what happened, yet." The officer took a step towards them.

"We found her, Bill." Charlotte looked at him. "When we left her, she was fine, then we went looking for Arnold and Peaches and tracked them here."

"You found them, obviously." Bill gestured to the animals.

"I know it's hard right now, but the more information we can get about Elisa, the better chance we'll have of catching her killer." The officer looked from Starla to Bill.

"I understand." Bill nodded slowly. "But I'm not sure how much we can tell you."

"We didn't really know her that well." Starla shivered. "She only worked here for a few months."

"That's all right." The officer crouched down beside her as she sat back down in the golf cart. "Whatever you can tell us about her will be helpful."

"There's not much I can tell." Starla wiped at her eyes. "She was a sweet girl, but she was a roamer. She told me she didn't like the idea of putting down roots."

"What about her family?" The officer met Starla's eyes as he spoke in a soft tone. "Is there anyone that we can contact about what's happened?"

"As far as I know, she didn't have any close family." Starla sighed, and her entire body trembled. "She was alone in the world, poor girl."

"She was alone because she wanted to be." Bobby crossed his arms.

"Why would you say that?" Charlotte turned her attention to Bobby. She'd been so focused on Starla's grief, that she hadn't noticed the tension in Bobby's muscles, or the clench of his jaw.

"It's true. She didn't get close to anyone." Bobby shrugged, his arms still tight across his chest. "If that was how she wanted to live, it was her choice."

"Maybe, but I'm certain that she didn't choose to die." Ally looked over at the shed, then back at Bobby. "Someone did this to her. Did you see anyone strange around on the farm? Anyone who didn't belong?"

"You mean other than you two?" Bobby lofted an eyebrow.

"Bobby." Bill frowned. "This isn't a time for joking around."

"No, it's not." Charlotte eyed him with some displeasure. She knew that everyone reacted to grief differently, but Bobby certainly seemed more angry than sad.

"Fine. No, I didn't see anyone. It was just the usual crew." Bobby turned away as the medical examiner's van arrived.

"I'm going to hang around a bit, but you shouldn't be here for this. Starla, let Bobby take you back to the house." Bill looked towards Bobby.

"You're right." Starla forced herself to her feet. "We're not doing anyone any good here. Do you want to ride back with us?" She glanced over at Charlotte and Ally.

"No thank you." Charlotte cleared her throat. "I think we'll walk."

"But it's so hot." Starla shook her head. "You shouldn't be walking in this kind of weather."

"Thank you for your concern, but I'll be fine. We need to take Peaches and Arnold with us anyway." Charlotte gave her a quick nod, then looked at Ally. "Shall we head back?"

"Yes, I think we should." Ally fell into step beside her grandmother as the golf cart darted off across the nearby field. "What are you thinking, Mee-Maw?"

"The way Bobby reacted, it just made me feel uneasy." Charlotte held tighter to Arnold's leash. "It's probably nothing."

"Maybe, but I doubt it. Your instincts are usually spot on." Ally glanced at her, then gazed down at the path as she continued to walk. There wasn't much that could be said to ease the shock of what they'd both experienced.

Even after they reached the car, and drove back towards Blue River, Ally remained mostly quiet. Charlotte turned into the driveway of the cottage, and Ally released a heavy sigh.

"Are we still going to open up the shop?" Ally asked. It was meant to be closed for the day, but if they could they would open it. The regulars loved it when they did.

"I think we should. If you're up for it." Charlotte looked across the car at her granddaughter. "We have a cake to make, remember?" She patted the top of the jar of jam that sat in the cup holder in front of the dashboard.

"Oh Mee-Maw, should we?" Ally frowned as she tried to figure out what was appropriate.

"Absolutely, we should. Elisa gave this to us, because she wanted us to make something delicious. I think it would make me feel a lot better, if we did just that."

"That sounds good. Let me just get Arnold and Peaches cleaned up, and we can head over." Ally herded the pets into the cottage and straight towards the bathroom. It took a bit of scrubbing, but she was able to get them all clean. She gave them both fresh water and food, then a light kiss on each of their heads. "I'll be home soon."

As Ally joined her grandmother in the car again, she felt a little better. When they reached the shop, her mood was bolstered a little more, just by the sight of it.

Once inside, Charlotte turned on some music in the kitchen. A large, glass window that faced the shop gave customers a full view of the candies being made, or at times, Charlotte and Ally dancing in the kitchen.

"Mee-Maw, this is exactly what we need." Ally began to gather the equipment to candy some of the fruit and dry some of it.

"I agree." Charlotte started on the white chocolate cake.

Within moments the two were immersed in the process of creating candy and cake. The music that filled the air brought some peace to Ally as she moved in time with it. The serene expression on her grandmother's face, soothed her even more. There was no way to make what happened that day better, but being together and doing what came most naturally to them, soothed it.

Once the fruit was candied and ready to cool, Ally headed to the front of the shop to open it. They wouldn't have the fruit candies ready until the next day. But there were plenty of candies ready to sell. As she turned the sign in the door to open, she noticed a shadow just outside the shop. She peered through the window, then smiled as she realized who it belonged to. She pulled open the door.

"Mrs. Bing, hi there." Ally smiled. "Oh and Mrs. White, and Mrs. Cale. Please come in."

"I was hoping you'd open soon." Mrs. Bing clutched her purse in her hands and looked into Ally's eyes. "We heard about what happened at the farm."

Ally held the door open for them and nodded as

they walked past. It didn't surprise her that they knew. Word spread fast through small towns, and Mrs. Bing always seemed to know everything about everyone. As she settled the three women at the counter with fresh cups of coffee, she heard her grandmother in the kitchen preparing another batch of candy.

"It's such a shame to lose a rock star." Mrs. Bing popped a chocolate into her mouth, then took a sip of her coffee. "Out of all of the people on that farm, why did it have to be her?"

"A rock star?" Ally leaned against the counter and studied Mrs. Bing's expression. The tension in her forehead and the tightness around her lips, made it clear that she had far more to say. "What do you mean by that?"

"Oh, just what I said. She was a rock star. Well, in my mind, anyway. She played with a group in Geraltin. She was new to the band and once she joined, they became very popular. The Geraltin Groovers." Mrs. Bing laughed and patted lightly at her chest. "I have no idea why they picked that name for their band. It seems like a band name for an older group of musicians, but I do enjoy the music."

"You enjoy the men!" Mrs. White rolled her eyes. "Every time they play a gig, this one just has to go." She shook her head as she leaned closer to Ally. "She's stalking a few of their fans as well."

"Stalking! Never!" Mrs. Bing gasped and shot a glare in Mrs. White's direction. "Sure, there are a few fellow fans that I enjoy spending time with, but I go there for the music. Especially the drums." She frowned, then picked up another candy. "I guess it won't be the same now, without Elisa on the drums."

"I had no idea she was in a band." Ally smiled some as she thought about the woman she'd met. "There's so much I don't know about her. I hope I have the chance to learn more."

"She was a very interesting person. I spoke to her a few times. I didn't know her very well myself, but she seemed tough, and talented." Mrs. Bing's chin trembled. "I only wish I could hear her play again."

"Oh Mrs. Bing." Ally covered Mrs. Bing's hand with her own. "I'm so sorry for your loss. I'm sure the police are working very hard to ensure that her murder is solved quickly."

"You can't be sure of that." Mrs. Bing drew her hand back and looked up at her with wide eyes. "Maybe if it had happened here in Blue River, you could be sure of that. Luke would certainly be on top of it, and I know he wouldn't quit until the crime was solved. But Geraltin? They're a bigger town. They have plenty of crimes to investigate. I doubt that they are going to put their full resources into the investigation." She sighed, then shook her head. "It's a shame, too, because I know exactly who killed that poor girl."

CHAPTER 5

 rs. Bing's words shocked Ally.

"What?" Ally stared at Mrs. Bing as her heart skipped a beat. "How could you know that?"

"Easily. That rotten neighbor of hers showed up at one of her last gigs. He stormed in, while the band was playing, and started banging two pot lids together. He jumped up on top of a table and banged them so loud that no one could hear the music. When the bouncer finally got him to leave, everyone clapped. Then Elisa explained that he was her neighbor, and that she was in an ongoing battle with him over her right to practice her music." Mrs. Bing clucked her tongue and scrunched up her nose.

"A terrible man. To come in there like that, to ruin everyone's good time, and to treat Elisa that way. I'm sure that if he was willing to do something like that, then he would be willing to take things even further and cause her harm. But do you think the Geraltin police will even look into him? I doubt it." She popped another candy into her mouth.

"She's probably right about that." Mrs. White nodded as she returned to the counter. "I hate to say it, but I've heard nothing but complaints about recent investigations in Geraltin. They have more resources than we do, but their case load is much larger, I guess. Still, that's no excuse not to do a thorough job."

"Hopefully, a dedicated detective is on this case." Ally glanced over at Mrs. Cale, who lingered near some of the wooden toys that Luke had recently carved. "Did you find something that you like, Mrs. Cale?"

"I think this one." Mrs. Cale smiled as she picked up a small car. "For my grandson, Kevin. Do you think he would like it? He might be a little too old for it."

"No one is ever too old for a hand carved toy." Ally walked over and took the car from her. "I'll box it up for you. I'm sure that he'll love it."

"Actually, I thought maybe if I paid a little extra, Luke might be willing to carve his name into the bottom? Do you think he would do it?" Mrs. Cale batted her eyes and offered a cherubic smile.

"Oh, I'm sure he'd be happy to." Ally grinned. "I'll take it to him tonight and I'll let you know when he can have it ready."

"Thanks so much, Ally." Mrs. Cale smiled.

"It's no problem. I'm sure Kevin will love it." As Ally placed it into a box, she heard Mrs. Bing and Mrs. White whispering at the counter. Curious, she edged her way closer to listen in. The two women weren't normally shy about sharing their opinions.

"You know he was in love with her. If he wasn't, then why did he show up to every single one of her gigs?" Mrs. White frowned, then drained the last of her coffee.

"I don't know, I've been to every one of her gigs, and wasn't in love with her." Mrs. Bing shrugged.

"Who do you think was in love with Elisa?" Ally picked up the coffee pot and held it out to Mrs. White.

"No thank you, I've had enough." Mrs. White sighed, then looked at Ally. "You know how I hate to point fingers. But wrong is wrong, and I think he might have had something to do with this."

"Who?" Ally set the coffee pot back down.

"Bobby." Mrs. White lowered her voice. "He worked at the farm with Elisa. He would come to every one of her gigs, at first."

"At first?" Ally held back a gasp as she tried to imagine burly Bobby caught up in a romance with Elisa.

"Yes, a few weeks ago, he showed up there with a bouquet of flowers before the show. He offered them to her, but she refused them, right in front of everyone." Mrs. White clucked her tongue. "I respect a woman's right to deny affection, but I thought she could have at least rejected him in private."

"How did Bobby react?" Ally asked. From the reckless behavior she'd seen on the farm, she guessed he might not be afraid to show his anger and he might have a bit of a temper.

"He just stood there. Then he turned around and walked out. Honestly, I thought there might be a bit more of a scene, but there wasn't." Mrs. White pointed to the peanut butter candies on the sample tray. "Can I get a box of these please?"

"Absolutely." Ally turned around and began boxing up the chocolates. As she did, she thought about Bobby. If he did have a crush on Elisa and she didn't return it, that might have been a good reason for him to attack her. He was also on the farm at the time of her death, while as far as she knew, her neighbor was not.

After Mrs. Bing, Mrs. Cale, and Mrs. White left, Charlotte came out of the kitchen.

"Are they gone?" Charlotte wiped her hands on a towel.

"Yes. I thought you might be hiding back there." Ally studied her. "Are you okay?"

"Yes, I just didn't feel like handling all of the questions. I did hear what they said about Elisa's neighbor, and Bobby, though. It sounds to me like Elisa had more possible enemies than we thought." Charlotte frowned. "The question is, which one killed her?"

"I don't know yet, but I plan to find out. Before I do that though, I want to make sure that the investigating detective is up to speed on all of this information. Would you mind taking over the shop for a bit?" Ally pulled off her apron.

"Not at all. Just call me if you need me." Charlotte glanced at the sample tray and grinned. "Looks like we need a refill."

"Yes, we do." Ally laughed as she rolled her eyes.

On her way to the Geraltin Police Department, Ally wondered if she really should visit the detective. Now that she'd heard so many rumors, she wanted to ensure that the detective had all of the information he could get. She doubted that he would turn down the extra information.

Ally turned into the parking lot and had to hunt for a parking spot. She'd never seen so many cars in the local police department parking lot, that was for sure. After she finally found a spot, she navigated her way through a crowd of people in front of the building, then stepped inside. The lobby was huge, and sparsely decorated. It gave her a sense of being inside of a hospital, or some other sterile environment. She took a deep breath and focused on her goal. All she wanted to do was talk to the detective, that was, if he would see her.

Ally reached the front desk and waited for the female officer behind it to speak. When she didn't, Ally spoke up instead.

"Hi, can I speak to the detective that is

investigating Elisa Price's murder, please?" Ally looked into the woman's vacant gaze.

"You don't know his name?" The officer shifted her attention to the computer in front of her.

"No sorry, I don't. But I may have some information for him. If I could just have a few minutes of his time, it might help." Ally glanced over her shoulder as a group of people entered the police station and began to fill up the remaining empty seats in the lobby.

"We're a little busy today. I can give you a form to fill out." The officer slapped a piece of paper down on the counter between them.

The coldness in the woman's tone was not lost on Ally. Still, she kept her voice friendly as she responded.

"Oh, thanks, but I'd really like to speak to him." Ally cleared her throat and smiled. "If it's not too much trouble."

"It is, because you don't even know who he is. We have several detectives on staff here." She sighed and her shoulders drooped. "I suppose I could look it up by the victim's name." She blew a bit of her hair away from her face and began to type on the keyboard.

"It's Elisa Price." Ally frowned as she noticed the apparently uncaring attitude of the officer.

"Okay got it. Right, that's Pauler. Okay, I'll see if he's available." The officer picked up the phone, pressed a button, then sandwiched it between her ear and shoulder. After a few seconds, she straightened up. "Hi Pauler, I have a visitor for you. She says she has some information about the Price investigation. Right." She paused, then narrowed her eyes. "No, that's Pride. This is the Price investigation. Elisa Price." She paused again, then looked at Ally with a shrug. "Do you want to see her or not?" She nodded then hung up the phone and jerked her thumb in the direction of a door to the side of the desk. "Go on back, he's the third office on the right."

"Thanks for your help." Ally met her eyes with a warm smile.

The officer shrugged and turned back to the computer screen.

As Ally stepped through the door, she found it was quieter in the hallway than it was in the lobby. Several doors lined it, and at the end was a large, open space with desks clustered together. Very few were occupied. She reached the third door and gave a light knock on it.

"Come in." The detective's gruff voice easily penetrated the thin door.

Ally pushed it open and stepped into the small office. "Detective Pauler?"

"Yes, that's me." He peered at her over wire-rimmed glasses. "What kind of information do you have for me?"

"Well, my grandmother and I were the ones that came across Elisa's body." Ally eased her way down into an old, rickety chair. For a second, she wondered if it would hold her weight. When it didn't collapse, she dared to take a breath. "I also recently found out that Elisa had quite a disagreement with her neighbor. I wasn't sure if you were aware of that."

"Elisa, Elisa." The detective began to sort through a thick pile of files on his desk. "Oh, that's a new case." He nodded as he pulled a folder out of the stack.

"Just this morning." Ally winced at his flippant attitude but steeled herself against judging the detective before she had the chance to get to know him. It was clear that he had a large caseload.

"I see. Uh huh." The detective glanced up at her. "Are you Charlotte or Ally?"

"Ally." She eyed the file, though she couldn't read its contents from across the desk.

"Okay, it looks like the officer at the scene took your statement. Who is this neighbor of hers?" Detective Pauler picked up a pen.

"I actually don't know his name." Ally shifted in her chair. "But according to a friend of mine, he showed up at one of her gigs and created quite a scene. I definitely think he's someone you should look into."

"He is?" The detective looked up, his eyes wide. "Well, that's good to know. It would be even better to know his name, don't you think?"

"Well, he's a neighbor. So, I think it's pretty safe to guess he's someone that lived next door to her." Ally narrowed her eyes but did her best to hold back her judgment. "It seems like a good person to look into."

"I'll look into it." The detective flipped the folder closed, then locked eyes with her across the desk. "Was there anything else that you wanted to tell me?"

"Actually, yes." Ally sat back and crossed one leg over the other.

"Oh no, don't get comfortable." Detective Pauler eyed her over his glasses. "I don't have time for you to get comfortable."

"I'm not comfortable, I promise." Ally shifted in the chair, which was remarkably uncomfortable. "There is someone else you may want to look into. I've heard a rumor that Bobby, a worker on the farm, might have had a romantic interest in Elisa." She watched as he sorted through his paperwork. "Aren't you going to write this down?"

"Like I said, I'll look into it." The detective flashed her a brief smile. "Anything else?"

Ally gritted her teeth to hold back sharp words. It wasn't her place to question his method of investigation, she realized that, but she wondered if he was going to investigate anything at all.

"What about the cherry pits? Did someone collect them and send them for testing?"

"I have no idea what you're talking about. All evidence at the scene has been processed, so if they were there, then yes." Detective Pauler shrugged.

"You seem to have a very large workload. I was wondering how many cases you are working right now?" Ally looked over the stack of files, then back at him. She did her best not to get furious over the way he spoke to her.

"I do. But rest assured, I will do my job, that's all that you need to know. Now, if you don't mind, every second I spend with you is a second less that I'm using to solve crimes." Detective Pauler gestured towards the door.

"I understand." Ally stood up from her chair, then paused. "Maybe you'd like to take my cell phone number? In case you want to ask more questions."

"That's not necessary, I doubt I'll need it." Detective Pauler flashed her a strained smile. "I'm sure it's in the case file, anyway." He reclined in his chair and folded his hands across his rounded stomach. "I hope you have a good day."

"Thanks." Ally stared at him. She hoped he would take the case seriously.

As Ally left the police station, she noticed several more people had entered the lobby and were standing along the back wall. She couldn't imagine how much work was about to be piled on to the officers. She was sure that they did their jobs, but how much time and energy could the detective dedicate to Elisa's case if he had several others to handle as well?

Ally settled in her car and stared through the windshield as she considered her options. She could just let it go, continue on with her day, and assume that it would all work out in the end. Or, she could look into the case further herself. There was no harm in giving the detective a helping hand, was there? With that in mind, she turned her car on. Before shifting into drive, she sent a quick text to her grandmother.

Can you find out what Elisa's home address is?

CHAPTER 6

*W*hile Ally waited for her grandmother to respond, she headed off in the direction of the farm. If Bobby was indeed in love with Elisa, or at least infatuated with her, then she wanted a chance to speak to him again. As it was, she couldn't be certain that Detective Pauler would ever get around to questioning him.

Flashing lights drew her attention to her rearview mirror. As soon as she saw the car reflected in the mirror, she smiled to herself. She signaled to pull over and guided the car on to the shoulder of the road. The unmarked car pulled up right behind her. She turned her car off and watched through the mirror as a handsome young man stepped out of the car. Detective Luke Elm didn't wear a uniform, but a casual suit, and his light brown hair was combed back neatly from his head. Sunglasses perched on the bridge of his nose. He walked towards her rolled down window and paused beside it.

"Where are you off to in such a hurry?" Luke rested his hands along the top of the car and bent down to peer inside.

"I don't believe I was speeding." Ally raised an eyebrow as she looked through the window at him. His stunning hazel eyes always took her breath away. "In fact, I don't believe there was any reason for you to pull me over."

"You're right." Luke offered her a slow smile that revealed a dimple in his cheek. "But I couldn't resist." He crouched down, bringing him to her eye level. "I heard about what happened out on the farm. Are you okay?"

"Yes, I'm okay." Ally smiled at him in return. "Glad to see you."

"You didn't even call." Luke frowned as he gazed into her eyes. "Why didn't you call me this morning?"

"I know, I'm sorry." Ally leaned close and placed a light kiss on his tense lips. "I knew you were working on a big case and I didn't want to bother you. I was going to call you around lunchtime, then I got distracted with everything and forgot."

"You know you can call me any time of the day or night. You are my first priority no matter what case I'm working on." Luke met her lips for another kiss and drew her as close as he could through the window. When he released her, he looked into her eyes again. "I just want to know what's going on in your life."

"I know, I'm sorry. I should have called straight away, but I got distracted. I wasn't really sure what happened. I mean, I know that Elisa is dead, but that's the most information I have." Ally searched his eyes. "You wouldn't know anything more than that would you? Anything about what happened to Elisa?"

"No, I'm sorry." Luke straightened up and brushed his hair back from his eyes. "Things are a little tense with Geraltin right now, I don't have too many connections. I'm a little friendly with the medical examiner, but I haven't heard anything."

"That's all right. I just thought I'd ask. Do you want to grab a coffee?" Ally tipped her head towards the passenger seat in her car.

"Sweetheart, I'd love to, but I can't. I have a

meeting back at the station. I can't miss it." Luke frowned. "Another time?"

"Of course, I understand." Ally gave his hand a light squeeze. "Listen, I need to bring something by to you tonight. Mrs. Cale bought one of your wooden cars, and she wanted you to carve her grandson's name in it. I told her you would, I hope that's okay."

"Of course, I'd be glad to. Why don't you let me make you dinner?" Luke smiled. "If you do, I'll let you go with a warning."

"I wasn't speeding." Ally grinned. "But yes, you can make me dinner tonight."

"Good." Luke leaned in for one more quick kiss, then headed back to his car.

As Ally pulled back out on to the road, for a few minutes she forgot about everything other than how lucky she was to be with Luke. But as she neared the farm, the memory of Elisa's death returned to her.

When Ally arrived at the farm, she noticed that it appeared just as busy as it had earlier in the day. She glanced around at all of the activity and wondered why the police hadn't treated the entire farm as a crime scene. The killer could have left evidence from the entrance of the farm all the way to the shed. But tractors rolled right over the paths he would have used. Maybe they had already processed the scene.

"Just who I wanted to talk to!" A familiar voice called out cheerfully to her from the front of the barn.

Ally turned and squinted through the sunlight. It took her only a second to figure out who it was.

"Christian." Ally walked towards him, her lips spread into a warm smile. "What are you doing here?"

"I'm covering the murder." Christian cleared his throat, then glanced over his shoulder. "At least I'm trying to. Not getting much traction around here."

"No one wants to talk to you?" Ally paused beside him and swept her gaze over him. Christian was fairly new to the area, he lived in Blue River and was a dedicated journalist, some might say a little too dedicated.

"Oh, they talk, but they have nothing to say. Everyone says they didn't know much about Elisa, and I can't seem to get a quote to save my life." Christian sighed, then locked his eyes to hers. "But now that you're here, maybe you can turn all of that around for me."

"How so?" Ally raised an eyebrow.

"I was going to catch you later at your cottage, but since you're here, I'd love to hear your account of how you found Elisa. Is it true that Arnold and Peaches made the discovery?" Christian poised his pen above his notepad and appeared to be ready to take down her every word.

"No, not really. They sort of led us to her. I'd appreciate it if you didn't use them in your article. It's bad enough that we lost track of them, and far worse that they could have been hurt by the terrible person who killed Elisa." Ally crossed her arms.

"Okay, okay." Christian held one hand up. "I thought it would be an interesting perspective, something to reach the hearts of the animal lovers out there, but if you're not okay with it, then I won't do it."

"Good." Ally tipped her head towards the trail that led past the barn. "Have you been up to the shed?"

"Not yet. Starla said someone would be coming by to give me a ride out there." Christian peered into the distance. "But I haven't seen anyone yet."

"That would probably be Bobby. You might want to step back." Ally gestured to the side of the trail as she heard the engine rev in the distance.

"Hmm?" Christian offered her a puzzled look, then his eyes widened as the golf cart raced towards him. "Hey, slow down!"

"It's okay, as far as I know he hasn't hit anybody yet."

The golf cart skidded to a stop right in front of both of them. Bobby flashed them a smile, then jerked his head towards the back of the cart.

"Hop in. It's the last ride of the day."

Ally stared at him for a moment. Was it wise to get into the golf cart of someone she now considered a murder suspect?

Christian didn't have any qualms as he climbed in. She did want to see the area around the shed again, and it would be a lot faster to take the golf cart. She also wanted to speak to Bobby, and this might give her the opportunity. Reluctantly, she climbed in beside Christian.

"You'd better hold on." Ally grabbed the frame of the cart with one hand.

"Huh? Why?" Christian settled back in his seat.

"Here we go!" Bobby stepped on the gas.

"Oh, I see!" Christian wrapped his arm around the other side of the frame and held on.

Ally, already used to the bumps and swerves of

the ride out to the shed, focused her attention on Bobby. He didn't seem particularly heartbroken over Elisa's death. But then again, if she had rejected him, maybe he no longer cared for her very much. Could emotions change so swiftly?

Bobby pulled up in front of the shed, and Ally continued to watch him.

"Are you going to stay here, Bobby?" Ally stepped out of the cart.

"No." Bobby spoke gruffly now and looked towards her.

"But I'll only be a minute, and I could really use the ride back." Ally offered him a light smile and hoped that he would at least look in the direction of the shed. A person's expression could be so telling, despite their attempts to hide emotions.

"I won't be far." Bobby winked.

The moment that Christian stepped out, Bobby slammed on the gas and took off into the field.

"Strange one, isn't he?" Christian smoothed down his shirt and glanced over the shed. "It doesn't look too daunting, does it? I don't know why but I always expect places where terrible things happened, to look just a little terrible."

"It looked pretty terrible this morning." Ally

swallowed hard as she gazed at the police tape that wrapped around the shed. At least someone had done that. "I have to check on something." She glanced over her shoulder towards Christian, only to find him taking pictures outside the shed. He didn't notice as she walked over towards the trees. After a quick search around she realized that the pile of cherry pits was gone. Either the police had taken them as evidence, the murderer had got rid of them, or someone else had found them. As she walked back towards the front of the shed, she caught sight of Christian as he looked at the screen on his camera.

"I got a few good pictures. But that's not going to do me much good unless someone starts talking about what really happened here."

"I'll tell you what I can, Christian, but it's not much. You might be better off investigating why Geraltin PD is so understaffed. That would be a good place to start at least." Ally couldn't disguise the annoyance in her tone.

"I'll keep that in mind." Christian offered her a small smile. "So, are you going to fill me in?"

Ally walked him through everything she could recall, but didn't get too vivid in her description.

She hoped it would be enough for his article, but she didn't want to belittle Elisa's death either.

"Thanks Ally, you've given me a lot to work with, and I will look into the Geraltin PD angle, too." Christian tucked his notebook back into his pocket.

"Please do. And let me know if you hear any tips. I'd really like to know what happened to Elisa." Ally stared at the shed as she heard the golf cart roar in the distance.

"Me too. I'm going to stick around for a bit and see what I can find out." Christian studied her for a moment. "Are you okay, Ally?"

"I'm fine." Ally glanced at him. "Thanks for asking, though. I just hope that Elisa gets the justice she deserves."

The brakes of the golf cart shrieked as it pulled up beside her.

"Ready to go?"

"Yes, I am." Ally slid into the passenger seat. If she was going to be alone with Bobby, she was going to take advantage of the opportunity to push him a little bit for information. As he shifted the golf cart into gear, she placed a hand lightly on his forearm. "Could you take it slow, Bobby? I'm feeling a little off at the moment."

"Sure." Bobby drove slowly down the trail.

Ally was a little stunned that he complied.

"Are you doing okay, Bobby? I know you must have known Elisa pretty well after working with her." Ally leaned back in her seat.

"Working with her? She didn't work with anyone." Bobby smirked, then shook his head. "Like I said, she didn't let anyone get too close to her. She was a private person."

"But you must have noticed someone around her. Didn't anyone call? Or come to visit her here at the farm?" Ally noticed the barn in the distance as they drew closer to it.

"No, nobody." Bobby shrugged and steered around a big hole.

Ally realized he could actually be a considerate driver when asked.

"I found out she was part of a band. Did you ever hear her play?" Ally knew this was a loaded question. Either he would lie, and indicate he had something to hide, or he would tell the truth, and reveal his affection for her.

"Yes, I heard her play. Many times." Bobby turned down the trail that led towards the barn. "I'll admit, she was good. I've heard better, but she was very good. I would go into town to hear her play at her gigs. I enjoyed the music. That was practically the only time she wasn't alone, when she was playing her music."

"I'm sure she appreciated you being there. It was nice of you to show her your support." Ally wished the ride would be a little longer, as he pulled up in front of the barn.

"I'm not sure that she saw it that way. But that's a nice thought. Have a good evening, Ally." Bobby stopped the golf cart. "I hope that you can get over this quickly. I know it must be rough for you."

"Thanks, Bobby. I appreciate your concern. I hope you're doing okay, too. If you ever want to talk about it —"

"I won't." Bobby smiled at her as she stepped out of the cart. "My policy in life is if it doesn't please me, then I don't pay it any attention."

As Bobby took off, Ally stared after him. Perhaps Elisa had stopped pleasing him, and the only way he could stop paying her any attention, was to make sure that she was gone completely. She couldn't quite place his feelings for her, but she suspected that Mrs. White's assumption about him was right. If that was the case, then Bobby had an awful lot to hide.

Ally's phone buzzed, drawing her out of the

dazed state she'd slipped into. She pulled the phone out as she walked towards her car. When she found the text from her grandmother, she smiled to herself. She had one more stop to make before she would head over to Luke's for dinner.

CHAPTER 7

*A*quick search of Elisa's address revealed
that she lived in a small rental home near
the center of Geraltin. Ally set her GPS to lead her
to it, and hoped that once she was there, she would
be able to discern where her disgruntled neighbor
lived. If not, she might just start knocking on doors.
Fresh determination rushed through her. She
needed to eliminate suspects so that she could focus
on Bobby more. At the moment she didn't have
anything more to go on than a good amount of
suspicion.

When Ally arrived at the house, she discovered
it was roped off with police tape. This surprised her
as she had begun to think that Geraltin PD wasn't
investigating at all. It also indicated that she would

not be able to get a peek inside. The last thing she needed was to be caught snooping around a crime scene. Besides, it wasn't Elisa's house she was interested in.

Ally scanned the surrounding houses for one that she thought might belong to her angry neighbor. It didn't take her long to pick one out. There were signs all over the yard beside Elisa's that declared the noise ordinance for the neighborhood, as well as lists of dates and times, and even a sign that featured a letter to Elisa that requested she find somewhere else to play her drums. It was clear that this neighbor had a huge problem with Elisa, and she doubted there could be more than one.

As Ally walked up to the door, she braced herself for what she might find. A few sharp knocks were answered within seconds by a man in gym shorts and nothing else.

"Yeah?" He leaned against the door frame. His eyes bloodshot as they surveyed Ally from head to toe.

"Sorry to wake you." Ally smiled briefly. "I noticed all of your signs, and I wondered if I might ask you about them."

"So, you noticed all of my signs, and still thought

it was a good idea to knock?" He raised his eyebrows. "Not very bright, are you?"

"Sir, I don't mean to disturb you. It's just that the woman that lives next door, she made arrangements to meet me, and now I see there is police tape around her house, and she isn't answering her phone. I thought you might have an idea of what happened and where she might be?" Ally glanced over the signs. "Since you seem to have a strong relationship with her."

"Strong relationship?" He chuckled, then stepped through his door and out onto the lawn. "Won't be needing these signs anymore." He plucked one from the soft dirt. "She isn't answering her phone because she's dead."

"Dead?" Ally took a step back as she feigned shock. "But she was so young. Do you know what happened?"

"Sure, somebody killed her. Probably somebody who was as tired as I was of her constant noise." He narrowed his eyes as he plucked another sign from the lawn. "When you move into a quiet neighborhood, it's just common courtesy to fall into place with the rest of the neighbors and live a quiet lifestyle. But that's not what she did."

"I see that you had a problem with her. How

loud could she have really been?" Ally crossed her arms casually across her stomach.

"Drums! She played those drums every single day and night, for hours. If she wasn't working, she was playing those drums. I went over there real polite at first, I said to her, hi there my name is Vick, I explained how this neighborhood is quiet, and that the neighbors are considerate of each other. I asked her to find another place to practice. But she refused. She just kept playing." He shook his head. "The police wouldn't do anything. They said that because she stopped playing by ten, she wasn't breaking any laws. But she was breaking my brain." He reached up and rubbed his hand along the top of his head. "I'm not sure how much more I could have taken."

"Wow, that does sound very frustrating." Ally bit into the tip of her tongue to keep from pointing out that there were a few methods he could have used to prevent himself from hearing the drums. It bothered her that it seemed as if he didn't care that Elisa was dead. "Still, it's a tragedy for someone so young, and clearly talented, to die." She watched as he plucked the last sign from the lawn. "At least you'll get a little peace now."

"Yes, finally." Vick breathed a sigh of relief. "You

know, I get it, no one should ever be killed. But I can't say that she'll be missed." He walked towards his garage. "If that makes me a bad person, oh well, I've never cared too much about things like that."

"I can understand why you're frustrated. It sounds like she wasn't a very reasonable person if she wouldn't tone down the drumming for you." Ally took a deep breath and continued to do her best to sound sympathetic. "I bet you weren't the only person she upset either. Did you ever see anyone in the neighborhood, or hanging around her house, that gave her a hard time?"

"A few of the other neighbors complained, but when I tried to get them to go to the police station with me, they chickened out." Vick glanced over at the house and stared for a moment. "I did hear an argument over there the other day. I was going to call the police about it, but it ended just as fast as it started, and the guy left. So, I figured there wasn't much point. It's not like the cops around here do much anyway." He rolled his eyes and tossed the signs into his garbage can.

"It was a guy? Did you happen to hear what they were arguing about?" Ally reached down to pick up one of the signs that had slid out of the garbage can.

"I don't know. I just heard shouting. He was a friend of hers, though. Uh, in the band. The guitarist, I think. I swear, he used to come over and play as loud as possible just to upset me." Vick snatched the sign from her hands and slammed it into the garbage can. "Like I said, you're not going to find me crying any tears over her. Now, if you don't mind, I'd like to go enjoy my peace and quiet." He gave her a short wave, then stepped back into his house. When he slammed the door shut, she jumped at the sound.

"Apparently you don't mind being noisy." Ally raised an eyebrow, then headed back towards her car.

Perhaps Vick was just nasty enough to kill someone over a noise complaint, he certainly seemed like he didn't have much of a conscience. The thought that things could escalate that far between neighbors disturbed Ally, but she knew it wouldn't be the first time it had happened. Would he go all the way out to the farm to kill her? That didn't seem like a crime of passion. He would have had to plan, and then execute it. Then again, perhaps he thought it would throw suspicion off himself if he made the effort to do it while she was at work. Ally was certain that he belonged on her list of suspects. But there was someone else that belonged on that list, too. She turned on her car and backed out into the street, determined to find out exactly why Elisa's bandmate engaged in a shouting match with her only a few days before her death. Close friends could make terrible enemies if things turned sour, and it sounded like things might have gotten very sour.

Ally made it back to the shop just in time to help her grandmother close it up.

"I'm sorry I was gone so long." Ally filled her in on all that she'd found out. "I really think Bobby is a good suspect. I think he would have had enough time to drop us off at the barn and go back to the shed and kill Elisa before we got there."

"He may be a good suspect, but there's also Vick, and now this guitarist?" Charlotte raised an eyebrow. "I'd say it's hard to pick which one is the most suspicious."

"You're right, but Bobby was the only one who was at the farm when Elisa was killed." Ally slid the last of the chocolates into storage for the next day.

"That we know of, someone else could have been

there." Charlotte tapped her chin. "I hope they get a new lead, quickly."

"I hope so, too." Ally frowned as she turned towards her grandmother. She then shared her frustrating experience at the Geraltin police department.

"Wow." Charlotte shook her head slowly. "I guess we do have reason to be concerned about this investigation being thorough."

"I think we do. I can't just sit back and let the leads go cold because Detective Pauler is too busy to look into them." Ally led her grandmother outside, then turned back to lock the door.

"It's quite interesting that she had a run in with her guitarist. Musicians can be so passionate about their work." Charlotte leaned her head back and took in a deep breath of the outside air. "If they were fighting over something, he might have snapped and decided to get rid of her."

"Yes, he could have snapped, but again, he would have had to plan the murder out. It's not as if he was at the farm with her." Ally paced slowly back and forth in the parking lot. "I think part of the problem is, we're not even sure exactly how she died. I noticed some cuts on her and assumed she had been stabbed. But thinking back, I'm not sure that I ever saw a wound big enough to be fatal."

"I don't think either of us looked too closely, we were both in such a state of shock." Charlotte shivered at the memory.

"You're right." Ally closed her eyes for a moment. "I wish we could see pictures of the crime scene. There is no way that anyone at the Geraltin police department is going to let me see them. But Christian took some pictures there today, maybe there's something in the photos that will reveal something. He couldn't get inside the shed, but I noticed him taking some photos around it. I had a quick look around but didn't notice anything I didn't see there before and most of the stuff had already been taken into evidence. But a close look at the photos might help."

"Maybe he'd be willing to let us see them." Charlotte glanced at her watch. "We need to get home and feed Peaches and Arnold. Oh, Mrs. Bing stopped by earlier to tell me that she organized a vigil for Elisa tonight at the Geraltin town square. Everyone in Geraltin and the surrounding towns are encouraged to attend."

"That's so thoughtful of Mrs. Bing. I'll take care of Arnold and Peaches, then meet you there." Ally adjusted her purse on her shoulder. "I mean, if you're up for it?"

"I was thinking we should definitely attend. If we can speak to the guitarist, we might be able to find out what the tension was between them. I'll see you there." Charlotte gave Ally a brief wave, then headed towards the van. Ally climbed into her own car and made the quick drive to the cottage.

After Ally fed Peaches and Arnold she freshened up, then sent a text to Christian to ask him about the pictures. It wasn't until her stomach rumbled that she recalled her dinner plans with Luke. As she did her phone beeped with a text. It was Luke apologizing. He had to cancel their date because he had to work. She replied immediately.

No problem. Going to the vigil for Elisa tonight. Love you!

Ally's thoughts returned to Elisa. She began to gather her purse and keys. Tonight, would be a night for all Elisa's friends to gather. As far as she knew she didn't have any family in town, or anywhere nearby for that matter. After only being in Geraltin for such a short time it wasn't surprising that she hadn't set down many roots. However, she did wonder if she had any close friends. According to Mrs. Bing, her band had quite a following, she guessed some fans would be at the vigil.

When Ally arrived at the Geraltin town square for the vigil, the crowd was far bigger than she anticipated. She decided to take a few minutes to learn as much as she could about Elisa. It might give her some ways to start conversations with her friends. She searched the internet for any information about Elisa. After a few attempts she came across a website dedicated to her band. A picture of all of the bandmates together drew her attention. Elisa was the only woman in the group, which consisted of her and three men. One had his arm draped around Elisa, with a guitar in the crook of his other arm. She guessed that this must be the guitarist that Elisa's neighbor had mentioned. She scrolled through the names beneath the picture.

"Axel Gant." Ally tapped a finger along her chin as she looked him over. He didn't appear to be dangerous, but then she wasn't quite sure what dangerous would look like. He was a slender man with long, curly hair and a bright smile. Elisa also looked content in his company. She tucked her phone away and stepped out of the car. If Axel was somewhere in the crowd, she intended to find him.

After about a half hour of searching, Ally realized it was going to be harder to find him than she thought. She'd come across her grandmother, and after chatting for a bit, she continued to look. But still no sign of Axel. Then suddenly the crowd parted, and a man walked towards her. She guessed that many of the people that gave him space recognized him and were fans of the band. Although it seemed as if he walked straight towards her, it was really only because she had yet to move out of the way.

"Axel? Can I speak to you for a second?"

He reached up and pulled off the sunglasses he wore, which was an odd choice at night.

"Who might you be?"

"My name is Ally. I was there at the farm today." Ally's muscles tensed as she continued. "I just wanted to say, I'm so sorry for your loss." She met his eyes as she offered her hand.

"Oh, none of that." Axel spread his arms wide and pulled her in for a tight hug. "I'm a hugger."

"Ah, I see." Ally smiled and returned his hug, then pulled gently away. "I can only imagine how hard this must be for you."

"It's rough." Axel ran a hand back through his long curls. She noticed a shimmer in them, as if he might have smeared some kind of glittery gel along the strands. "She was young, and so talented. Really, just a gift to the world."

"I'm sure you two were very close." Ally looked into his eyes again, in search of any flinch or glimmer that might indicate discord.

"We were at times, and not at others. Being in a band is like being in a family. You fight like cat and dog, but you always stick together, you're part of something." Axel glanced over his shoulder in the direction of the other members of the band. "It's going to take a lot for us to recover from this."

"Do you plan to continue the band?" Ally followed his gaze. "Maybe playing her music will help with the loss?"

"Her music?" Axel's head snapped back in her direction. "What do you mean by that?"

"I saw on your website that she wrote most of the songs for the band, so I just assumed that you might want to continue to use those songs, or maybe any works in progress that you might be able to find." Ally shrugged but noticed that his lips drew into a rigid line.

"She claimed to have written all the songs since

she joined the band, and she's the one who published the website, that's why it says that. But I wrote all of the songs before she joined and we co-wrote only a couple together, and she knew that. I did most of it." Axel crossed his arms as his cheeks reddened. "It doesn't matter now. From now on we'll be playing my music, just like we always have been. If you'll excuse me." He tipped his head towards a group of people gathered near the candles. "I should speak with a few people."

"Of course." Ally nodded, then turned to watch him walk away.

"That sounded a little rough." Charlotte stepped up beside her. "Was he as angry as he seemed?"

"Not at first, but once I mentioned the songs being written by Elisa, he got quite upset. He claimed that he wrote them." Ally looked over at the rest of the band. While they remained clustered together, she hadn't spotted any of them looking in Axel's direction. He didn't seem overly concerned with them either, as he made his way through the crowd gathered in honor of Elisa.

"Interesting. Perhaps that's what the argument with her was about." Charlotte shrugged.

"Deceit can certainly be a strong motive." Ally nodded.

CHAPTER 8

When Ally finally arrived at home, she was exhausted and was excited to be greeted by Arnold and Peaches at the door.

She dropped her keys in a bowl on the table near the front door. As she stretched her arms above her head, she tried to clear her mind. It was obvious to her that there were a few suspects to consider. Elisa had no shortage of people upset with her, despite only being in the area for a short time. There was Axel, who insisted that Elisa lied about who wrote the songs they played. He clearly had a temper, and didn't seem completely heartbroken over Elisa's passing.

Then there was Elisa's neighbor, who seemed like the type who could possibly snap. She couldn't overlook the possibility that Bobby had been overwhelmed by heartbreak either. With so many people to consider, she knew the main problem was that she had no idea who Elisa was. Perhaps if she had the chance to get to know her better, she would have a clearer feel of who might have wanted to hurt her. As it was, she could only recall that Elisa seemed kind, and intelligent. Nothing about her indicated that she had people after her. And yet she'd ended up dead, only minutes after she and her grandmother had left the shed.

Ally kicked off her shoes and crawled onto the couch. Peaches crawled up beside her and nestled into her favorite spot, the slope of Ally's stomach. Ally trailed her fingertips down through the cat's fur as she tried to sort through all of the possibilities in her mind.

"What do you think, Peaches?" Ally scratched behind her ear. "Did you see who did this to Elisa?"

Peaches stretched out her paw and pushed it against Ally's stomach. She looked into her eyes and gave a soft meow.

"I know. You saw something." Ally sighed and stroked her fur again. "I just wish that you could tell me what you saw. Maybe then we would know which way to turn." She considered all of the options she had for getting to know Elisa better. She doubted she would get any other information out of her neighbor, and she had no idea if Axel could be trusted. As for Bobby, she didn't want to believe that the man who gave her two terrifying rides on a golf cart could have been a murderer. He seemed generally cheerful, but the way he whipped the cart around the farm indicated he was also reckless. He wasn't forthcoming with information. She doubted that he would even talk to her again, but if he did, she didn't think she could trust what he had to say. There were two people that she knew of in Elisa's life that might be able to tell her more, Bill and Starla.

They claimed that they didn't know Elisa very well, but they had been on the farm with her for a few months. That meant they had to know something. She couldn't imagine Elisa never saying a word to either of them about where she came from, or friends or family members that meant something to her. She decided to invite Bill and Starla to the shop the next day.

As Ally pulled out her phone, Peaches stuck her nose up to the screen and meowed.

"There's no one on the other end, silly." Ally smiled and patted the top of the cat's head. She was about to text her grandmother when she saw there was a text from Christian with some of the photos from the shed. She slowly browsed through the photos and cringed as they brought the memory of finding Elisa's body to the surface.

Nothing in the photos stood out to her until something in one of them caught her eye. She noticed there was a piece of paper on the ground by the window outside the shed. She swiped her fingers to enlarge the screen and realized it was a flier advertising a performance for The Geraltin Groovers. She hadn't noticed it at the shed before but doubted it meant anything. She looked through the rest of the photos but found nothing that seemed out of the ordinary.

Ally texted her grandmother about inviting Bill and Starla to Charlotte's Chocolate Heaven the following morning. Charlotte replied almost immediately that she was having breakfast with Jeff and she would be late but told Ally to still set up the meeting as she would try to join them.

Ally called Starla's number and put the phone to her ear. As it rang, she wondered if it might be too late to call her. She knew that farmers tended to wake very early, so she doubted that she stayed up very late.

On the third ring, Starla answered the phone.

"Hello? How can I help you?"

"Hi Starla. It's Ally Sweet. I just wanted to check on you."

"Oh Ally!" Starla's voice cracked with excitement. "I'm so glad to hear from you."

"I didn't see you at the vigil tonight, I thought maybe I missed you." Ally continued to pet Peaches.

"Actually, Bill and I didn't go. It's just been such a terrible day. I wasn't up for getting in the middle of a big crowd. Bill doesn't like those sorts of things. You understand, don't you?"

"Of course. Completely. Are you doing okay now?" Ally frowned as she wondered how Starla was handling all of the stress.

"So far, so good. I needed a little time to myself, and luckily I got it."

"I'm glad you did." Ally reached down and patted Arnold as he stretched out by her feet.

"I actually called to invite you and Bill to the shop tomorrow morning. We made some cake and chocolates with the jam and fruit. If you're up for it, I mean."

"That would be fantastic. Thanks Ally. I'm not sure if Bill can make it, but I'll be there."

"Great."

"See you in the morning, Ally."

After Starla ended the call, Ally considered texting Luke. But she decided against it. He was obviously busy. Surely, he would contact her when he had some free time.

After stumbling through her nighttime routine, Ally finally crawled into bed.

The next morning, Ally woke up to Peaches kneading the space between her shoulder blades. Ally peered at her through one open eye.

"I don't mind a massage, Peaches, but you really should at least wake me up first."

As if to show she understood, Peaches flopped her tail right into Ally's face.

"Mmph. Thanks." Ally brushed her tail away, then sighed as she remembered the day before. She had to get up and get ready to open the shop. But all she wanted to do was go back to the moment that she left the shed, and stay. Just stay, for however long it took to make sure that Elisa was safe. But if someone was waiting for her to be alone, it might not have made a difference. She couldn't help wondering about the woman she barely knew and hoped that Bill and Starla would have some more information to share about her.

When Ally finally climbed out of bed, she felt

the weight of the day before on her shoulders. She moved through a shower sluggishly, then headed for the kitchen. Peaches was right there on the counter. She perked up when Ally walked into the kitchen, and with a not so subtle meow let her know that she expected to eat.

"Just a second, Peaches." Ally reached into the cabinet for Peaches' food, then sidestepped to avoid tripping on Arnold. Only Arnold wasn't there. She was so used to the pig eagerly waiting at her feet to be fed that she anticipated it even when he wasn't in the kitchen. "Arnold? Aren't you hungry?"

The pig waddled his way into the kitchen, his nose to the ground. He didn't dart, like he normally would at the slightest chance of food. He just crept his way in, then flopped down on the floor beside Ally's feet.

"What's the matter, Arnold?" Ally peered down at the sleepy pig. "Didn't you get enough rest last night? Or did Peaches keep you up?" She glanced over at the cat who prowled across the counter. "Did you try to play with Arnold's tail again?"

Peaches sniffed the air, then turned her back towards Ally.

"Well, I can't leave you two alone if something is up with you. I guess you're coming to the shop with me today. Maybe you can help cheer Bill and Starla up." Ally loaded the animals into the car, then headed off to the shop.

When Ally arrived at the shop, she left Arnold and Peaches in the courtyard behind it, then headed inside. She settled into the routine of opening the shop. Since her grandmother had turned it over to her, she had taken a lot more responsibility around the shop. But it still didn't feel like a job to her. Being there, felt more like home than anywhere else ever had, aside perhaps from the cottage where she had grown up, and now lived in again. She felt very lucky to be able to love her home and work as much as she did.

When Ally heard a light knock on the door of the shop, she turned to find Starla outside. She smiled and walked over to unlock it. It was a bit early to open up, but she decided to turn the sign to open and leave the door unlocked, in case any regulars wanted to come in. With only a few pieces of fruit candy and white chocolate raspberry cake to hand out, she planned to share them with her regular customers, like Mrs. Bing, Mrs. White, and Mrs. Cale.

"Hi Starla."

"Sorry, I'm a bit early."

"No problem. My grandmother is running late, she might not be able to join us."

"Thanks for inviting me. Bill couldn't make it, too much to do on the farm, as usual." Starla took a deep breath of the coffee-scented air. "That smells delicious."

"Coming right up." Ally winked at her and walked around behind the counter. "Just brewed."

"You really know how to brighten up my day, Ally." Starla settled on one of the stools at the counter. "I didn't think that was possible today."

"I know it must be so difficult for you." Ally set a hot cup of coffee down in front of Starla.

"It is. I just keep thinking how Elisa had no one here that was close to her. She was estranged from her family. It's hard to fathom that she had no family in her life." Starla looked across the counter at Ally.

"Maybe that was why she came here. Maybe she wanted to set down roots." Ally poured herself a cup of coffee as well. "Since it looks like she didn't have roots elsewhere."

"I'm not sure. Elisa never mentioned any of it to

me." Starla sighed. "I wish I knew more about her. At least something that could help."

"Here, I want you to be the first to try these." Ally set out a sample tray of the fruit candies and cake.

"I can't believe you made some already." Starla sighed with pleasure as the candy melted in her mouth. "Oh my, this is so good. The way the chocolate mingles with the fruit is just delightful."

"I hoped you would like them." Ally smiled. "My grandmother and I were so eager to get into the kitchen. We really wanted to try it out. It felt like we were honoring Elisa in a way. It's such a shame that we only have a small batch of them, and not many people will be able to try the cake with the raspberry jam, because we only have one jar."

"I'm sure Elisa would have loved these." Starla shifted on the stool and rested one elbow on the counter. "You know, Bobby knows how to make the jams. If you still wanted to order some, I'm sure he would be willing to make it for you."

"Oh?" Ally's eyes widened. "I didn't know that. Did Elisa teach him?" She wondered if that might have been how they grew close.

"No." Starla laughed a bit, then leaned closer to Ally. "He's the one that taught her, actually. It's his family recipe. He's been doing it for years. He gives jars of it away for the holidays. But it was Elisa's idea to try to sell the jam. That's why I gave her a promotion and let her run the business. That kind of initiative is priceless. It's the kind of thing that I like to encourage in my employees."

"Wait a minute, are you saying that Bobby got passed over for a promotion because Elisa turned his idea into a business?" Ally's brows knitted together.

"Yes, sort of, you can look at it that way. No one is ever guaranteed a promotion on our farm. If you do hard work, if you come up with inventive ideas that can potentially make the farm more money, possibly a lot more money, then I'm going to reward that. Bill never worries about that side of things. He works such long hours on the farm. I have to make sure that the farm makes money." Starla lifted one shoulder in a shrug. "Unfortunately, not everyone is concerned with helping the farm succeed. Bobby is a great guy, he works well with every employee we've had, and he's always willing to do the dirty jobs. But that doesn't bring us in any money. He was never very ambitious. If I start handing out promotions and business opportunities, just because I like a person, then we're not running a business anymore."

"That's a good point." Ally nodded, though her mind spun with thoughts of how angry Bobby might have been when he found out that someone who had only been on the farm for a few months was promoted ahead of him. And was using his recipes. Add that to the fact that it appeared as if Elisa had rejected his romantic interests, and it was a recipe for murder.

A scratch at the back door drew Ally's attention.

"Oh, that must be Arnold. I brought him and Peaches in with me today. Would you like to say hi?" Ally smiled as Starla stood right up.

"Absolutely I would. He's my favorite pig." She grinned.

"Great, he probably knows you're in here." Ally walked her to the door and opened it up.

"Hi there, Arnold." Starla crouched down to have a good look at him. She ran her hand back across the top of the pig's head. "You know, Ally, he's not looking so good." She looked up at Ally as she stepped through the door behind her.

"He's just a little worn out." Ally crouched down beside him as well. "He had a lot of exercise yesterday. I think once he gets some rest, he will look much better."

"I don't know, he just looks so gray." Starla shook her head as she studied him. "You might want to keep an eye on him."

"I will." Ally frowned. She was sure that Starla was used to working with animals. If she thought something was wrong with Arnold, then there really might be. After Starla left, Ally decided to call her grandmother, as a sick feeling began to grow in the pit of her stomach.

"Mee-Maw, I think we need to get Arnold to the vet."

"Oh dear, why, is something wrong?"

"He's just not acting like himself. I just had coffee with Starla, and she mentioned that he didn't look well either. I don't know, it's probably nothing, but I would feel better if he was checked out." Ally glanced up at the clock.

"I'll take him. I'm just around the corner with Jeff. Arnold hates going to the vet. Trust me, he'll figure it out, and he'll have a fit. I'll be there in just a few minutes to pick him up. I'll bring Jeff along in case I need the back-up."

"Okay Mee-Maw, thanks." Ally ended the call, then eyed Arnold again. "What's the matter, buddy?" She crouched down and patted his back. "Did you get into something you shouldn't have?"

Arnold looked up at Ally and blinked. Then he dropped his head again. He sprawled out on the ground and gave a sad squeak. She frowned as she studied him. Had she been so distracted by the murder that she missed Arnold getting sick?

CHAPTER 9

"*A*lly?" Luke's voice carried through the shop. "Are you in here?"

"Yes, I'm here." Ally stepped back from the door and poked her head out of the kitchen.

"I'm sorry about last night." Luke walked towards her.

"That's okay, we can have dinner later in the week."

"Of course, and I completely forgot about the wooden car."

"Right!" Ally smacked her forehead. "I also completely forgot about that."

Luke followed her out to the register. She handed him the box with the car in it.

"Kevin. I wrote the name on the box for you."

"Thanks." Luke leaned back against the counter beside her. "Listen, I did hear some information about the investigation today. But this has to stay between us."

"What is it? Do they have someone in custody?"

"No, not even close." Luke shook his head. "But the preliminary results from the medical examiner have come in. Apparently, Elisa was poisoned."

"Poisoned?" Ally narrowed her eyes. "But that doesn't make any sense. I saw cuts on her."

"From what I was told, their best guess is that she fell into glass jars as she was overtaken by the poison, but it was the poison that killed her not the cuts." Luke glanced towards the door as Mrs. Bing stepped inside, then lowered his voice. "They are trying to determine the source of the poison. It could be anything."

"Anything?" Ally repeated the word as Mrs. Bing sneaked up to the counter and picked up a piece of white chocolate raspberry cake that Ally had left on the sample tray. In that moment Ally realized that the jam had come from the farm, and had in fact come from the same shed that Elisa died in. Wasn't it likely that it could be poisoned? She lunged forward and smacked the cake out of Mrs. Bing's hand.

"Ally!" Mrs. Bing gasped as she took a step back. "I would have paid for it!"

"It's not that, Mrs. Bing." Ally winced as she realized how hard she slapped the woman. "That cake isn't safe. Please, don't eat it."

"It's not safe? How can it not be safe?" Mrs. Bing narrowed her eyes. "Do you just want to keep it all for yourself?"

"No, Mrs. Bing." Ally opened her mouth to explain, but a light squeeze from Luke's hand on her wrist reminded her that this was not to be public knowledge. "It's just a bad cake, it doesn't taste right. I'll get you some of your favorite chocolates from the back." Ally grabbed the fruit candies and cake off the counter. She wasn't going to take any chances.

"Okay, thank you." Mrs. Bing rubbed her hand and eyed Ally with distrust.

Luke followed Ally back into the kitchen as she began to pack up all of the cake and fruit candies.

"Did you or Charlotte eat anything while you were at the farm?"

"We tasted the jam. But that was it." Ally frowned. "I'm feeling fine, and as far as I know, Mee-Maw is, too. I'm sure it was safe."

"It might be a good idea to get checked out just in case." Luke frowned.

"What is there to check out? I don't have any symptoms." Ally looked towards the back door, and her heart dropped. "But Arnold does."

"Arnold?" Luke followed her gaze towards the door. "What's wrong with him?"

"He's lethargic and looks a little gray." Ally opened the back door to show him.

Arnold barely lifted his head, and gave a light snort, before he closed his eyes again.

"This is terrible, Ally. We need to get him to the vet." Luke started to crouch down to pick him up. Ally's heart softened at how Luke had learned to love Arnold. The feeling was definitely mutual. Coming from the city Luke had been very apprehensive about the pig when he first met him.

"It's all right, Mee-Maw is coming to take him. He doesn't like going to the vet, so it's best if she takes him." Ally spared him a small smile. "Thank you for wanting to help, though."

"Always. Arnold is my little pal. What about Peaches? How is she feeling?" Luke glanced around for her.

"As sassy as ever. She ate her breakfast and she's

relaxing out back." Ally shook her head. "That cat knows how to get the best treats in town."

"Ally?" Mrs. Bing called from inside the shop. "Are you still back there?"

"Yes Mrs. Bing, I'm coming right out." Ally gave Luke a light pat on the shoulder then headed out to Mrs. Bing with some fresh samples. As she poured her a cup of coffee she wondered if Arnold might be sick from poison. He had been digging in the dirt by the shed. Both animals had gotten some jam on them. Had Arnold ingested some of the poison? Her heart pounded at the thought.

As Ally handed Mrs. Bing her coffee, she recalled that Starla had eaten a few candies and cake earlier that morning. She pulled Luke aside.

"Starla was here and ate some of the fruit candies and cake. What if she's sick, too?" Ally looked into his eyes. "Can you check on her for me, please?"

"Of course, I can. I'm sure she's fine, though." Luke straightened up, then paused. "Remember, this needs to stay quiet. If it gets around town, the medical examiner will know that someone leaked the information."

"I'll remember." Ally nodded. "But we may need

to tell the vet that there is a chance Arnold ingested poison."

"That's fine, you do what you have to do to get Arnold better." Luke leaned close and kissed her cheek. "Please let me know how he is doing."

"I will." Ally watched him walk through the door.

"He is one tall drink of water." Mrs. Bing smacked her lips. "And these candies are delicious."

"I'm glad you like them." Ally offered her a brief smile. Her thoughts returned to Arnold, just as her grandmother pushed open the door. Jeff was close behind her.

"Where is he?" Charlotte's voice was filled with tension that came from fear. "We need to get him in the car right away. I brought some treats."

"I'm not sure he's going to want to eat them. He didn't touch his breakfast this morning." Ally led her to the back door.

"Oh, that's not good!" Charlotte sighed. She pushed open the door and spotted the pig in the grass. "Arnold, what's wrong, sweetheart?" She dropped down to her knees beside him, then wrapped her arms around his neck. "Don't worry, Dr. Blake will get you all fixed up."

"Are you sure you don't want me to go with

you?" Ally watched as Jeff picked Arnold up in his arms. "I could shut the shop down for a little while."

"I'm sure it's nothing. Let's keep the shop open for now." Charlotte looked over at Ally. "I'll make sure he gets better. I have Jeff with me to help if I need it."

"Mee-Maw, there's something I need to tell you." Ally kept her voice down as she relayed the information that Luke had given to her. "We have to keep it to ourselves as it's part of the investigation, but the vet may need to know."

"This is worse than I thought." Charlotte gritted her teeth, then followed after Jeff as he carried Arnold to his car. "It's okay, buddy, we're going to make you feel so much better."

Charlotte sat in the back with Arnold. He lay still and barely lifted his head when they went over a bump. She knew from experience that he was sick. Arnold never liked to be still. Now and then he would curl up for a nap, and he enjoyed sitting across her lap, but in general some part of him remained in motion. At the moment, he didn't move a muscle.

Jeff turned into the parking lot of the veterinary clinic. Charlotte's heart was in her throat. Arnold had been a part of her life for so long, a loving and uplifting part. He gave her such joy, and the thought that he could be seriously ill made her chest ache with fear. Gingerly, Jeff gathered him in his arms, and carried him inside. As soon as they stepped through the door, Arnold started to squirm in an attempt to get out of Jeff's arms. He gave a half-hearted squeal and looked frantically in the direction of the door.

"It's all right, Arnold, Dr. Blake is going to help you." Charlotte gently stroked Arnold's back as Jeff did his best to prevent him from breaking free. It appeared that even though Arnold was not feeling well, he had gotten stronger when faced with the prospect of seeing the vet.

"Charlotte!" The veterinary nurse, Erin, a young man with wide eyes and a wider smile, rounded the desk. "Dr. Blake is waiting for you and Arnold, you can head right back." He leaned close to take a look at Arnold. "How are you feeling, buddy? A little under the weather?"

"I'm afraid so." Charlotte frowned as she recalled what Ally had said. Was it possible that Arnold had been poisoned? If so, then minutes might make a difference in his treatment. "We need to get back there right away, Erin, I'm sorry." Charlotte followed Jeff as he carried Arnold into the exam room, where she found Dr. Blake in the act of putting on her gloves.

"Jeff, go ahead and put him on the table." Dr. Blake walked towards them as Jeff set the pig down. "He certainly does seem lethargic, usually he's fighting you tooth and nail when he's here." Dr. Blake clucked her tongue.

"He did try to make a leap for the door." Charlotte coasted her palm down along the top of Arnold's head, and continued to caress across his back. "But he is just not himself, Dr. Blake. I have to tell you, there may be a possibility that he ingested something dangerous." She glanced towards the closed door, then lowered her voice as she looked back at Dr. Blake. "Maybe even poison."

"Poison? Like a pesticide?" Dr. Blake began to run her hands along Arnold's frame. Then she checked his heartbeat.

"No, not necessarily. Actually, I have no idea what it might have been, but it is a possibility." Charlotte sighed.

"Hm." Dr. Blake listened to Arnold's heartbeat again, then shined a light into his eyes. After a moment of trying to get Arnold to be still enough to get a good look at his eyes, she changed her focus to his mouth. "Open up for me, buddy." She coaxed the pig, then spoke to Charlotte. "If he did get into something that he shouldn't have then he might have some sores in his mouth." She sighed as Arnold jerked away from her. "Without knowing what's happening with him, I don't want to take the risk of sedating him. Can you give me a hand, Charlotte?"

"Sure." Charlotte frowned as she wrapped her arms around Arnold's neck and did her best to hold his head in place. "Sorry, buddy." She whispered to him, and kissed the top of his head. Arnold peered up at her with a look of betrayal in his eyes that threatened to break Charlotte's heart. "She's only trying to help you, Arnold."

"Let's see." Dr. Blake peered inside of Arnold's mouth. "Interesting. There are a few small sores and some redness." She looked up at Charlotte, again. "You have no idea what he might have been exposed to?"

"I'm sorry, no. I don't." Charlotte blinked back tears as she thought about the possibility of Arnold being poisoned. Perhaps if she had been more careful with him, if she had kept a better eye on him, instead of trusting that he would be safe with Starla, she might have prevented all of this from happening.

"I'll take a swab and see if I can find anything out from that." Dr. Blake frowned as she released Arnold's mouth. "But to be honest with you, Charlotte, there isn't much I can do without knowing exactly what he might have ingested. I can give him a general treatment that will hopefully help with any toxins that are currently in his system, but without more information I can't be certain that it will work."

"I understand. I wish I could tell you more, but I just don't know. Please Dr. Blake, do everything you can to help him." Charlotte fought tears that threatened to spill down her cheeks.

"I will." Dr. Blake gave Arnold a light pat on the back. "That I can promise you. But it might be best if you left him with me at least for tonight. I want to keep a close eye on him and monitor any changes. Hopefully, whatever he got into isn't too serious."

"I understand." Inwardly, Charlotte trembled. If Arnold had gotten into something that contained the same poison that killed Elisa, then it was undoubtedly very serious. She wrapped her arm around Arnold and pulled him close. "I'm sorry, buddy, I know you're not going to like staying here, but it's for the best. Dr. Blake is going to take very good care of you, and I'll be back to check on you as soon as I can."

"If anything changes, I'll be sure to let you know right away." Dr. Blake peered into Arnold's eyes. "You and me tonight, hmm? We're going to figure out what's going on with you."

"I sure hope so." Charlotte pressed her hand to her chest.

"He'll be in good hands." Dr. Blake brushed her hand along one of his hooves. "Huh, what's this?" She lifted his leg up enough to peel away a small piece of paper stuck to his hoof.

"I'm not sure what that is. He must have picked it up somewhere." Charlotte touched the edge of the paper, then frowned. "Ugh, it's sticky. It must have been at the farm. He was rooting around in some of the jam that had spilled into the dirt at Starla's farm."

"I'll toss it out." Dr. Blake started to turn towards the trashcan.

"No wait, may I have it?" Charlotte reached for the paper.

"Are you sure that you want it? It's pretty grimy." Dr. Blake held it out to her and shrugged.

"Yes, thank you." Charlotte grabbed the corner

of it. "It could be evidence, since it might have been at the crime scene."

"Good point." Dr. Blake pulled a small, plastic bag out of a nearby drawer. "Here, so you can keep it safe."

"Thanks, Dr. Blake." Charlotte tucked the piece of paper inside the plastic bag, then leaned over to give Arnold a kiss on the top of his head. "I'll be back later to check on you, Arnold."

"I'll be here, whenever you want to stop by." Dr. Blake patted Arnold. "Don't worry, Charlotte, I will make sure he is comfortable."

"Thank you." Charlotte couldn't even look at Erin as she left the office with Jeff. As soon as they reached the car, she burst into tears. The last thing she wanted to do was leave Arnold behind, but she knew there was nothing that she could do for him. He was in the best hands he could be. Her focus needed to be on finding out what happened to Elisa, so that she could help Arnold.

After Jeff gave her a hug and assured her that everything would be okay, Charlotte wiped her eyes and took a few deep breaths. Then she turned her attention to the potential evidence that Dr. Blake found on Arnold's hoof. She peered through the plastic bag at the paper. With a few wipes of her fingertips through the plastic she managed to clear away enough of the sticky substance to see some of the writing on the paper. It looked as if part of the writing had been torn off.

"Look at this, Jeff." Charlotte showed him the paper. "It was stuck to Arnold's hoof."

"Really, I wonder what it is."

'Sal' in printed fancy red letters and 'Geraltin Groovers' was scribbled on one side. A bolt of recognition caused Charlotte's eyes to widen.

That was Elisa's band. She turned it over. There was a four-digit number written on the back. 'Two six four two.' What was Sal and what did the numbers mean?

$\mathcal{A}$lly did her best to prepare some chocolates for a big order due the next day, but she found it hard to concentrate. When her cell phone rang, she lunged for it and answered immediately.

"Is he going to be okay, Mee-Maw?" Her heart pounded as she waited for the answer.

"I'm not sure yet, Ally. I do know that Dr. Blake is going to do everything she can to help him. He has to stay overnight for observation." Charlotte sighed.

"Oh Mee-Maw, you sound exhausted." Ally winced.

"I'll be all right, Ally. I'll be better once Arnold is home. We need to put our heads together and figure this out." Charlotte explained about the paper stuck to Arnold's hoof.

"You're right. The paper is interesting, but how would he get that on his hoof?"

"I'm not sure. My best guess is that it was on the ground near the shed."

"Maybe. I must have missed it when I cleaned Peaches and Arnold. I really just washed his face and body. I was going to give him a proper bath outside when I had more time."

"I'm not sure that it will have anything to do with the investigation, but I kept it, just in case it might lead to something. Ally, I'm terribly worried about Arnold."

"So am I." Ally released a heavy sigh. "I wish there was something I could do."

"If we don't find out what poison Arnold might have ingested, then he might not get better." Charlotte's voice wavered. "Dr. Blake tried to sound positive, but I could tell that she was very concerned. I just don't know what to do."

"Try not to worry too much, Mee-Maw. I know how much you love Arnold, I love him, too. He's strong, and he will get through this." Ally's heart fluttered, she hoped that was the case. She had no way of knowing if Arnold would improve or not.

"I'm trying. Dr. Blake said that if we knew what kind of poison was used, she might have a better chance of helping him. I wish Luke was working the case, I know he would do whatever he could to find out that information for us." Charlotte huffed. "I'm guessing that Detective Pauler would not be the least bit interested in the well-being of a pig."

"I doubt it." Ally frowned as she recalled the generally indifferent detective. "You should go home, Mee-Maw, I can handle the shop."

"No, I'd rather be there. I need to have something to do, something to keep me busy. I'll see if Jeff will stay with me, he's good at keeping me calm." Charlotte took a breath, then cleared her throat. "Ally, I don't often get scared, but this time I am. I'm sorry, I want to be strong for you, but every time I think of Arnold, I just want to cry."

"It's okay, Mee-Maw. You don't have to be strong for me. We're going to figure this out."

Ally ended the call and did a search on her phone to see if there was any more news about the murder. The first headline was, 'Jam Maker Poisoned'. Ally quickly skimmed the article to check if the type of poison was mentioned. It wasn't. She searched other news sites but there was no mention of the murder. She texted Christian to see if he knew anything about the poison. He replied that he didn't. She tried calling Luke to see if he had any new information about the type of poison. The call went straight to voicemail.

Ally finished packing up the chocolates, as she considered her options. Sitting still and waiting, was not one of them. As her mind cleared, a plan surfaced. When her grandmother arrived at the shop, with Jeff in tow, she grabbed her purse and keys.

"Mee-Maw, I'm going out for a bit."

"Wait." Charlotte spun around as she was barely in the door before Ally headed through it. "Ally! You stop right there!"

Ally froze on the step, then turned slowly back to face her grandmother. She hadn't heard that tone of voice in quite some time.

"What is it?"

"You're up to something. I know that look on your face. I want you to tell me what it is." Charlotte crossed her arms as she locked eyes with her granddaughter.

"I think you'd better tell her." Jeff raised an eyebrow as he stood about a foot away from Charlotte.

"It has been reported in the news that Elisa was

poisoned, but not the type of poison used. Just keep your phone on, Mee-Maw. As soon as I find out what the poison was that killed Elisa, I'll call you. If I'm not back before closing just leave everything for me to clean up. Okay?"

"Ally, what are you going to do?" Charlotte narrowed her eyes as she gazed at her granddaughter.

Ally sighed as she realized she wasn't going to get away from her grandmother that easily. "I'm going to find out the information that we need. No matter what it takes." She stared back at her grandmother for a moment, daring her to argue. When it came to a battle of wills, they tended to be equally stubborn.

"Just be careful." Charlotte caressed Ally's cheek as she held her gaze a moment longer. "Okay?"

"I promise." Ally nodded, then hurried out through the door. With her heart in her throat she rushed towards her car. Arnold was in trouble, and she needed to find out what had made him sick.

Just before she got to her car, a cat ran up to her. She crouched down to pet the white cat with light brown patches.

"Cinnamon." Ally smiled as she ran her hand

over the cat's back. Cinnamon used to be a stray that Carlisle, an elderly man who lived down the street and generally kept to himself, had taken in. Cinnamon ran off towards home and Ally, feeling a little calmer, walked towards her car.

As Ally drove in the direction of Geraltin, Luke's words echoed through her mind. He'd warned her that the medical examiner wasn't releasing any details about the poison, but she had to try. She loved Arnold as much as she loved Peaches, and she knew her grandmother loved him even more. If that was possible. He was more than a pet, he was family. She needed to do everything she could to help him.

As each mile passed on her way to Geraltin, she felt more pumped up, more determined. The wind left her sails as she pulled into the parking lot of the medical examiner's office. How exactly was she going to convince the medical examiner to tell her anything? She took a deep breath and stared through the windshield at the one-story building. She took another deep breath and reached for her phone. In that moment it began to ring. She saw that it was a call from her grandmother and picked it up.

"Mee-Maw, is everything all right?"

"Yes, sorry to scare you, Ally. I just wanted to let you know I'm going to close up early. I want to be with Arnold for a little while before the vet clinic closes."

"Oh yes, I understand completely. I just arrived at the medical examiner's office. I will let you know what I find out."

"Ally, I trust that you know what you're doing, and I love you." Charlotte ended the call.

Ally hoped that she'd be able to come through for her grandmother, and for Arnold.

Once Ally had tucked her phone back into her purse, she headed inside. The office itself was small, despite the building being quite large. A stern looking woman sat at the front desk. She wore a pair of glasses that seemed almost too large for her face.

"May I help you?" She stared at Ally with a smile that managed to be polite and grim at the same time. Was it ever appropriate to smile at the morgue?

"I hope so." Ally cleared her throat. "I really need to speak with the medical examiner. I know it's late in the day, but is there any chance that I could speak with him?"

"Her." She pointed to a picture on the wall

behind the desk. In it, a woman who looked to be in her forties with short, red hair gazed out over the office. Her stern expression indicated that it was in fact, not ever appropriate to smile at the morgue. "Dr. Gene. She isn't available for appointments this afternoon, but I could schedule you something for tomorrow."

"That's not going to work." Ally placed both hands on the counter and looked into her eyes. "I need to see her today. In fact, I need to see her right away."

"She has assignments." The receptionist gestured towards the hallway. "She's tied up for the rest of the afternoon. There's nothing I can do for you. Would you like me to take your name and number down?"

"Please." Ally's mind spun as she tried to come up with an excuse urgent enough to speak to the medical examiner. She realized that trying to explain Arnold's predicament would likely not get her very far. Instead, she decided to pretend to be him. "I'm sick." She cleared her throat. "I'm very sick. I think I've been poisoned." She grabbed the counter as she began to sway back and forth. "I know that you have the victim here, the one that was poisoned, and I need to know what the poison was." She fixed her with a desperate gaze. "Please, I need to know right now!"

"Wait, you think you have been poisoned?" The receptionist jumped up from her chair and reached for the phone on her desk. "I'll call an ambulance right away."

"No, there's no time for that!" Ally gulped out her words as she tried to think of a lie before she could get to the phone. "I need to know what the poison was, or I won't survive. I've already been to a doctor, and he said there was nothing he could do without knowing what it was. All I need is just a minute of the medical examiner's time! Please!"

"Wait, a doctor thinks you've been poisoned, but he let you leave the office? Why didn't he send you to the hospital?" The receptionist walked around her desk and grabbed Ally's arm to steady her. "What kind of doctor was this?"

"An acupuncturist actually." Ally's head continued to spin with panic as she wove whatever story she could come up with. "What does it matter? Just get me the information!" She wobbled her way to a chair as the receptionist guided her.

"I'll see what I can find out. You just sit here for a moment." The receptionist gave Ally's hand a light pat, then rushed towards the hallway.

Ally didn't have to pretend to be out of breath. All of the pressure left her breathless. She knew that her story wouldn't last long. It was easy to see through, and once she was examined it would be clear that she was perfectly healthy. But she hoped that in the urgency of the moment she would get the information that she needed.

When a figure emerged from the hallway, Ally could tell right away that it wasn't the receptionist. The woman with short, red hair was tall, and her broad shoulders amplified her size. As she approached Ally, she wore the same expression she had in the photograph that hung behind the desk.

"Who are you?" She stopped short in front of Ally and crossed her arms.

"Please, I'm so sick. I just need to know what kind of poison killed Elisa. I don't have much strength left." Ally swayed in the chair.

"What newspaper do you work for?" The medical examiner leaned forward on her toes and tilted her head down until she was face to face with Ally. "I want your name, I want your ID, and I want you to know that I will be speaking to your boss and demanding that you be fired."

Ally's stomach flipped as she realized that the

woman wasn't buying an ounce of what she was selling.

"I'm not a reporter." Ally cleared her throat and eased up from the chair, though did her best to maintain a bit of space between herself and Dr. Gene. "That's not why I'm here."

"Then why are you here?" The medical examiner glared as she crossed her arms. "Wasting my time?"

"You're right, I'm not sick." Ally took a breath and did her best to soften her voice. "But someone I love very dearly is, and if I don't find out what kind of poison he ingested, he might not survive the night."

"Then his doctors should have called me to ask." Dr. Gene took a slight step back and eyed Ally with skepticism. "I haven't received any calls."

"He's not exactly a person." Ally frowned as she continued. "He's a pig. My grandmother's pet, and part of our family. He helped find Elisa's body, and I'm afraid that he ate the same thing she did, and has been poisoned as well. Please, I know it's not normal for me to ask this. I know that you may not think a pig is very important but —"

"Nonsense, I adore pigs." Dr. Gene's arms

settled back at her sides. "I have one at home. Are you sure he has been poisoned?"

"I'm not. He has just been acting strangely today, he won't eat and is lethargic. He has sores in his mouth." Ally bit into her bottom lip.

"When did he start to feel sick?" The medical examiner asked. "Was he okay yesterday? Did he eat?"

"This morning he wouldn't eat." Ally frowned. "He was fine yesterday."

"How did you know that Elisa was poisoned?" The medical examiner stared at Ally.

"I saw it on a news site."

"The news?" Dr. Gene raised her eyebrows.

"Yes."

"Well, the details of the poison will probably be released soon, but you need to keep this to yourself." Dr. Gene frowned. "Okay?"

"Of course, I just need to help Arnold." Ally nodded.

"It isn't possible that he was poisoned with what Elisa was. If he had any of that poison at all he would have got very sick straight away." The medical examiner frowned.

"But he has mouth sores and he's not eating?" Ally sank back down into the chair behind her.

"Maybe so, but they were not caused by what killed Elisa." The medical examiner shook her head. "I do hope that your pig will get better quickly."

"Thank you." Ally's heart pounded as she attempted to process the information that she had been given. If Arnold wasn't sick from poison, what else could it be?

Dr. Gene turned around to leave, then suddenly turned back.

"I recognize you now."

"You do?" Ally's heart stopped for a second.

"Detective Luke Elm's girlfriend." Dr. Gene smiled slightly. "I've seen you two together. I guess he doesn't know you are here."

"No." Ally's heart stopped for a second. "I couldn't get hold of him and I needed to help Arnold."

"I see." Dr. Gene nodded.

"Thank you for your time, Dr. Gene, I really do appreciate it." Ally smiled.

"You should." Dr. Gene quirked an eyebrow, then walked back down the hallway.

Ally gave a short wave to the receptionist before she hurried out the door.

CHAPTER 11

*A*lly climbed into the car and pulled out her cell phone. She wanted to tell her grandmother what she'd learned, as soon as possible.

"Pick up, Mee-Maw. Pick up." She counted down the rings and expected it to go to voicemail. At the last second her grandmother answered.

"Ally, I'm sorry I was just in with Arnold. Did you find out what kind of poison was used?" Charlotte's voice was hopeful.

"Mee-Maw, I managed to speak to the medical examiner in Geraltin. I have good news and bad news." Ally took a breath as she started the car.

"What's the good news?" Charlotte's voice trembled. "Is it good for Arnold?"

"It could be. I'm not sure. Dr. Gene said that the poison that killed Elisa was fast acting. If Arnold had come in contact with it, it would have affected him straight away and much worse than it already has. So, he has likely not been poisoned and definitely not by the same poison." Ally sighed as she backed out of the parking lot. "Unfortunately, that doesn't tell us what is wrong with him."

"Oh, that pig." Charlotte groaned. "I know what is wrong with him! He has a belly ache! He probably ate up all of the jam that spilled out under the shed door. That would explain the sores in his mouth, too, as he is sensitive to strawberries. I can't believe I didn't think of that. Ally, I'm going to let Dr. Blake know right away. The shop is all closed up, and everything is settled for the night. You can go straight home."

"All right, Mee-Maw, thank you. Let me know what the vet says. I hope it really is just a belly ache and an allergy, that would be such a relief." Ally ended the call and turned down the road to head in the direction of Blue River. Her thoughts shifted briefly back to Dr. Gene, and how she might know Luke. Would she tell Luke that Ally had come to speak to her? She guessed that it would only be a matter of time before she mentioned it. It would be better if Luke heard it from Ally first. She veered off her intended path and headed instead for the Blue River police department. As she neared it, she wondered how he might react. She knew Luke well enough to expect him to be calm, and logical about the situation. Still, a sense of dread brewed within her. She parked, then headed inside.

It was quiet, there weren't many people in the lobby. A dazed officer stared into space behind the front counter.

"Ally?" Luke's voice drifted over her shoulder from a few steps behind her.

"Luke." Ally smiled as she spun around to face him. All it took was his voice, the sight of him, or even a text from him to cause that smile.

"I imagine you are here to see me." Luke crossed his arms as he met her eyes. "Maybe there's something you intend to tell me?"

"Uh, yes." Ally shivered as she realized that he must already know. "Did you talk to Dr. Gene?"

"Yes." Luke sighed and caught her by the elbow. "Let's talk outside."

"When I saw that it was in the news that Elisa had been poisoned, I tried to get hold of you," Ally explained.

"I know you did. I was in an interrogation."

"I'm sorry, Luke, I couldn't wait. I had to speak to Dr. Gene. I had to do something. I had no choice." Ally tried to catch his eye as he led her around the corner of the building.

"I know, because of Arnold." Luke released her arm and pressed one hand against the brick wall. "I know how worried you were about him. Sorry I couldn't take your call earlier. The only reason I know that you spoke to Dr. Gene is because I called to find out the information about the poison myself." He finally met her eyes.

"You did?" Ally bit into her bottom lip.

"I hoped she had gotten some results in. I thought I would try for you and Arnold." Luke leaned closer to her as his voice softened. "Luckily, Dr. Gene has a soft spot for pigs, and was willing to help."

"Luckily. I'm so relieved." Ally sighed.

"I know." Luke swept his hand from the wall, to the curve of her lower back and pulled her close to him. "Everything is going to be okay."

"Is it?" Ally rested her head on his shoulder.

"It is. I'm glad Arnold is going to be okay. I'm glad that you and Charlotte are not in any danger from the poison." Luke brushed a few strands of her hair back behind her ear. "Now, I need a kiss to celebrate."

"You're silly." Ally laughed. The relief of Arnold not being poisoned, gave her a subtle buzz of excitement. She leaned in and kissed him. For a few seconds she lost herself in the bliss of his taste and warmth, but as she pulled back, the pressure of the investigation rushed back into her mind. "Luke, I need to know who did this to Elisa, and how she consumed the poison. What do you think it could have been?"

"Anything." Luke shrugged. "The jams, fruit, coffee. Anything. It's hard to say. I'm sure Geraltin PD will test everything they found in the shed with her."

"Look at you, you're not getting any rest, are you?" Ally reached up to brush her fingers through his ruffled hair.

"I do have a big case." Luke gazed into her eyes. "Are you saying I look tired?"

"I'm saying, you need a home-cooked meal and a good shoulder massage." Ally raised an eyebrow. "Tempting?"

"So very tempting." Luke sighed, glanced over his shoulder in the direction of the police station, then looked back at her. "But I'm on call until tomorrow. Maybe then?"

"Absolutely then. I'm a little occupied, too." Ally stroked his cheek. "Once the killer is caught, I hope that we'll both have some more free time."

"Me too. But looking into this isn't safe. You need to be careful." Luke glanced at his watch. "I have to get back to work. Let me know how Arnold's feeling. All right?"

"Yes, I will." Ally leaned close for another kiss. As a ripple of passion inspired her to wrap her arms tighter around him, a thought crossed her mind. Did Elisa and Axel or Elisa and Bobby ever have that kind of relationship? "I'll talk to you later." She kissed him again, then headed back to the parking lot. Luke was a level-headed, kind man. She trusted that he would never do anything to hurt her. Could Elisa say the same of Axel and Bobby?

In the back of Ally's mind, she was aware that she was hungry. Also, tired. Also, she really wanted to spend some time with Luke. But all of that swirled just out of her focus. Her thoughts were mainly on Elisa. What was her life really like? Why had she really come to Geraltin? If Ally knew anything, it was that people usually didn't make big moves in their lives without a reason, and those reasons were often secrets. She had her own reasons when she returned to Blue River, heartbreak, and a loss of direction. What had driven Elisa?

A few quick searches on the internet again revealed that she didn't have a lot of information out there. She guessed that she was a private person but maybe she had confessed something to her friends. Perhaps, she had confided in her bandmates. Even if she hadn't, they might have noticed something about her that could help. She placed a call to Ken, the lead singer.

"Who is this?"

"Hi Ken, it's Ally. We met at the vigil for Elisa?"

"Oh yes, Ally." Ken cleared his throat and smoothed out his voice. "How are you?"

"I'm okay, thank you. Could I speak with you? Maybe I could meet up with you and Nick?" Ally braced herself for possible rejection. Would a couple of musicians want to spend time with someone like her? She lost her cool factor a long time ago.

"Sure, I'll let him know."

As Ally set up a time with Ken, she hoped that it would lead to more information about Elisa. She also hoped that Axel wouldn't get wind of the meet-up and try to join in. She could recall his arrogant nature and guessed that he would be quick to tilt the conversation in the direction he preferred. Luckily, both men were available right away, she hoped meeting them at the diner so quickly would prevent Axel from getting involved.

CHAPTER 12

When Ally arrived at the diner, she was relieved to see that only the two men were waiting for her. She joined them at a small table.

"See, I told you it was the chick from the vigil." Ken rolled his eyes.

"I remember you now." Nick nodded as he looked her over. "So, why are you really here?"

"Just to chat with you." Ally looked between each man, then shrugged. "I suppose if I'm being honest, it's really because I wanted the chance to get to know Elisa better."

"Oh." Nick lowered his eyes, then shifted in his chair.

"She was such a cool girl." Ken sighed as he

sank down in his seat. "I still can't believe she's gone."

Nick and Ken ordered sodas and Ally ordered a coffee, then she turned her attention back to the men.

"Had she been acting strange at all lately? Afraid, or upset?" Ally looked between the two. If there was an issue with Axel would they even mention it?

"Not really. Well, there was one thing. She came home one night, late, with a whole pile of paperwork. We were supposed to rehearse, but she told us to leave. She gave us an updated performance schedule so she must have been by the bar on the way." Ken rubbed his hand across his short, dark hair. "I remember because I was pretty annoyed. I'd blown off a date to be there. She took ages to get home, then told us to leave."

"Yeah, that's right." Nick nodded and crossed his arms. "We tried to convince her to practice at least a little bit, but she refused. When I asked her what was so important, she wouldn't tell me a word about it. She practically shoved us out the door."

"Right." Ken nodded, then stifled a yawn. "It was the strangest thing. But we didn't know her that well. I just figured it was her thing to be distant and rude all of a sudden. Some women can be like that."

"I suppose so." Ally gritted her teeth and held back her thoughts on making a comment like that. The important thing was, what did Elisa bring home with her?

"The next day she was killed. I wish I had known something." Nick balled his hands into fists. "Anything that would have saved her."

"Me too." The third voice came from about a foot away from the table.

Ally looked over her shoulder as Axel made his way to the empty chair beside her.

"Axel." Ally's heart sank. That was it, she knew the other men wouldn't be as talkative with him around.

"I guess I wasn't invited to the party." Axel raised an eyebrow as he spun the chair around backwards, then sat down on it. "Did you lose my number, Ally?"

"I just didn't want to disturb you. I know you must be going through so much right now." Ally locked eyes with him. "But I'm glad you're here."

"Me too." Axel tipped his head towards the other men. "Don't you two have somewhere to be?"

"What? No." Ken frowned.

"Really? Nowhere?" Axel chuckled. "What about that job I got you two hired for?"

"Oh man!" Nick jumped up from his chair. "Was that today?"

"Yes, it's today." Axel glanced at his phone. "And it starts in ten minutes."

"Ugh, I can't believe I forgot." Nick gave Ally a quick wave. "Sorry, another time maybe."

"Sure." Ally sighed as she watched the two men take off.

"I guess it's just you and me now." Axel folded his arms across the top of his chair, then rested his chin on them. "So, why are you really here, Ally?"

"I'm just trying to get to know Elisa better. I didn't have the chance to while she was alive." Ally looked into his eyes.

"But you didn't ask me." Axel shrugged as the drinks were delivered. "That's strange to me."

"I know that you two had been fighting lately." Ally lowered her voice and leaned a little closer. "Her neighbor told me. He heard you two arguing."

"Ah, I see." Axel nodded slowly. "And that makes me a murderer?"

"I didn't say that." Ally frowned as she took a sip of her coffee. "I just didn't think you'd want to discuss her with me."

"That argument, it was just a stupid blow up we had about the band. I told her she should stick her nose back in her books because that was where she belonged." Axel lifted his shoulder in a half shrug. "She didn't like my tone, I guess."

"You guess?" Ally raised an eyebrow as he had a sip of the soda that was meant for one of his bandmates. "It sounds like it was quite an argument."

"We ran hot and cold. Sometimes a little too hot, and sometimes a little too cold. But she could dish it out as good as me." Axel crossed his arms and leaned back against the wall. "I can see you judging me. You think I was a terrible bandmate."

"I'm not judging you." Ally narrowed her eyes just enough to hide the twitch in them. Could she disguise the fact that there was a little bit of judgment? "I'm only interested in learning more about Elisa. Were you two dating?"

"No way, not anymore anyway. We did date a few times when she first joined the band. But everything just died down." Axel shook his head. "We were just bandmates."

"What did you mean by get her nose back in her books? Was she a student?"

"No, not that I know of, that was about what she

used to do. She was an accountant. When she moved here, she joined the band, and I grilled her about her past. When she admitted that she used to be an accountant, I thought it was hilarious. I mean how do you go from a button-down kind of life like that to playing drums in a band? It doesn't make much sense, does it?" Axel grinned.

"It's unexpected, that's for sure. It sounds like she wanted to make a very big change in her life. Did she ever mention why? Was she running from something?" Ally made a mental note to dig deeper into her past. There had to be something there to find, and when she did find it, it might lead her in the direction of Elisa's killer.

"I don't think so. If she was, she never mentioned it. All she said was that she was bored, painfully bored. Her parents wanted her to go into accounting like they were, but she hated it. That was all I really knew about her past, she did tend to avoid talking about it. Maybe it was because I teased her too much, but I think it was more likely because she just didn't want to talk about it." Axel ruffled his hand back through his hair and held back a yawn. "Now, I've got these cops asking me all kinds of questions. I don't know, I guess I feel a little guilty that I didn't know her better. I should have known her better."

"It can be overwhelming to be questioned by the police." Ally nodded slowly. "But I'm sure you've given them all of the information that you can. Don't be so hard on yourself."

"I'm trying not to be, but when they look at me with all of that expectation in their eyes, as if I'm supposed to give them the information to somehow solve the crime for them, I just don't know what to say." Axel leaned towards her some. "They want me to confess you know."

"Confess?" Ally's eyes widened as she took a sharp breath. "Do you have something to confess to?"

"No, of course I don't. But they don't believe that. Every time I open my mouth they are hanging on every word, waiting for me to trip myself up. It's exhausting." Axel looked into her eyes. "Aren't you friends with a cop or something?"

"Sort of." Ally looked back at him and noticed the shift in his expression. It was subtle enough that she could have missed it if she hadn't been paying such close attention. But once she saw it, she couldn't un-see it. He was attempting to manipulate her. "Why?"

"I thought maybe you could talk to him for me. Maybe put in a good word." Axel shrugged. "I wouldn't want the police wasting their time chasing down false leads."

"He isn't involved in the case at all. Right now, I'm sure that you're one of their best leads. You knew Elisa very well." Ally sought his eyes as he glanced away. "Maybe you didn't kill her, Axel. But you might just hold the key to finding out who did. That's not something that they are going to give up on." She finally caught his gaze and held it. "It would be best if you cooperated with them."

"I am!" Axel huffed and closed his eyes. "I am telling them everything, but they don't believe me. It's like they won't be happy until I confess to the crime. What could I possibly tell them, that they don't already know?"

"Maybe that you were there that day. When Elisa died. You were on the farm." Ally watched as his eyes flew open. After seeing the flier beside the shed in the photo that Christian had given her, she had a hunch that Axel was there the day Elisa was murdered. If she pretended, she knew he was definitely there, he might reveal the truth. She locked her gaze to his. "Weren't you?"

"Yes, I was there." Axel rubbed his hand across

his chin and frowned. "I went there to try to talk some sense into her, to keep the band together. She was going to ruin everything, she wanted to leave the band. I brought her some fliers I had made, so she could see how serious I was about continuing our gigs. But imagine my surprise when I discovered that she wasn't alone."

"What do you mean?" Ally's eyes widened. "Who else was there?"

"Bobby." Axel's jaw clenched as he shook his head. "I knew that cowboy was no good when I met him. When he started hanging around her all of the time, I warned her. I told her to be careful of him, that he wanted more than friendship. She told me I was crazy." He shoved his hand into his pocket and rolled his eyes. "I saw the two of them together. They were sitting close together and staring all lovingly into each other's eyes. I tossed the fliers and took off. I didn't want to get into the middle of that. That was the last time I saw her. Okay?"

"How can I believe you?" Ally's heart pounded at the thought of Elisa and Bobby being involved in some kind of romantic interlude shortly before her death. "You didn't tell any of this to the police, did you?"

"No, I didn't. It would have made me look just a

little guilty, don't you think?" Axel quirked an eyebrow. "Jealous ex kills the woman he loved? But I didn't love her. We were just having fun. We just went on a few dates. I'm not going to jail over her bad taste."

"Axel." Ally smiled slightly. "Bobby was teaching Elisa how to make jam. You probably misunderstood what you saw. They were probably just working together."

"You think she was so innocent?" Axel chuckled and flicked a piece of paper in her direction. "Think again." He stalked off, his gait quick and sharp.

Ally bent down to pick up the paper. It was a picture. Bobby and Elisa sitting next to each other, gazing into each other's eyes. She stared, stunned, at the image that gazed up at her. Her heart skipped a beat. It could be completely innocent, but it appeared that they looked longingly at each other.

With the knowledge that Axel and Elisa had dated, and seeing the photo of Bobby and Elisa, Ally drove towards the cottage. Her grandmother planned to meet her there. and with this new evidence, she needed to talk out some new theories. Had Bobby killed Elisa because he was jealous of Axel, and if he couldn't have her no one could? Had Axel killed Elisa because he was jealous of Bobby, and if he couldn't have her no one could? Each possibility held water, but not much.

When Ally arrived at the cottage, she found the van parked in the driveway. She stepped inside, greeted by the scent of lemon and ginger tea.

"Oh Mee-Maw, this is just what I need, thank you." Ally smiled and threw her arms around her grandmother. "I am so glad that Arnold is okay."

"Me too. But I keep thinking about him there without me." Charlotte sighed and closed her eyes. "I know he'll be fine. I trust Dr. Blake. She said she would stay with him, which is very kind of her. But what if he needs me, and I'm not there?"

"I know, Mee-Maw." Ally took her grandmother's hand and smoothed the palm of her other hand over it. "I know this is stressful. I wish he was here with us, too. But at least we know that he hasn't been poisoned. I bet by tomorrow he'll be back to his curious self."

"I hope so." Charlotte took a deep breath. "I suppose we need to focus on Elisa. It looks like whoever did this, knew just what to do, what poison to use, and how to deliver it."

"Which is way more than we know." Ally sat back in her chair and frowned. "It may take ages to find out how the poison was administered. And who killed her. That's plenty of time for whoever killed Elisa to make an escape or cover up their crime."

"I know." Charlotte nodded. "I've been thinking about Elisa. She seemed like such a kind person, yet she had quite a few people upset with her."

"Between her neighbor, Bobby, and Axel I'd say she certainly did. But I'm not sure that any of that was her fault." Ally considered what Axel revealed to her, then pulled out the picture to show her grandmother. "Not only did Axel lie to the police about the last time that he saw Elisa, but he also lied about the fact that they had been dating. I don't think that Bobby has been telling the whole truth either. It looks like Mrs. White was right and a lot more was going on between Bobby and Elisa than just learning how to make jam."

"Interesting." Charlotte picked up the picture and looked it over. "This doesn't really prove anything. But that gives Axel even more possible motive, doesn't it? If he had this, then he knows about their relationship. Jealousy probably got the better of him."

"He claims they just had a few dates, he wasn't jealous. He was trying to get Elisa to stay in the band, that he and Elisa were just friends, and there was nothing serious between them." Ally shook her head. "I can't be sure of that. He doesn't seem the type to be head over heels in love with anyone but himself, however."

"Hmm." Charlotte tapped her fingertips on the picture. "But that doesn't mean it didn't offend him that these two were together. Arrogant men don't like it when someone challenges their perfect image."

"True. But he seemed to be honest with me about their relationship." Ally tapped her finger on her chin.

"I don't think we can rule him out as a suspect, yet, but I also don't think that we should rule out Bobby. We don't know much about him, and what we do know indicates that he felt the need to hide his relationship with Elisa." Charlotte tipped her head back and looked at the ceiling. "So maybe, he taught Elisa the recipe, thinking that they were going to be together. Maybe she decided to end it. Or Bobby discovered that she had feelings for Axel, and he caught the two of them together?"

"Maybe." Ally frowned. "I think I need to have another conversation with Bobby."

CHAPTER 13

*E*arly the next morning Ally woke with a start. Her mind immediately drifted to Arnold. She stretched and wiped her hand across her eyes. Before she could sit up, her cell phone buzzed on her bedside table. She turned over and grabbed it in time to see a text from her grandmother. Instead of words, she had sent a picture. Arnold gazed into the camera, his eyes bright, and his ears perked up. He looked perfectly healthy.

A rush of relief flooded Ally. She texted her grandmother back quickly.

He looks amazing. Bring him home anytime you like. I have an errand to run this morning but I will be there in time to open up the shop.

With Arnold on the mend, there was nothing holding Ally back. She wanted to know the true relationship between Bobby and Elisa. So, she was going to focus on Bobby. He could be the key to the truth of what happened to Elisa. As she set her phone back down, she drew her knees to her chest and thought about the best way to get the information that she wanted from Bobby. He didn't seem like the type of person that would be forthcoming with information. He appeared straightforward, and she guessed that he would reject any attempt she made at getting the information from him.

After a quick shower she took some time to feed Peaches, then set out on her mission. As she drove towards Bill and Starla's farm, it occurred to her that she had no idea what she might walk into. Would there be a police presence? Would Bobby even be there? If he was, would she be able to find him? It didn't take her long to find out, once she'd arrived. She parked her car near the barn and noticed Bobby right away. He stood not far from the entrance of the barn, with Bill at his side. At least, he started out at his side, then he stalked a few feet away. Bill spun on his heel and turned back to Bobby, his cheeks flushed. Ally eased the window down in her car and caught a few of the words exchanged between them.

"It's best to cooperate with the police and tell them the truth, Bobby."

"Best for who? You? That's easy to say when there are no fingers pointing at you!"

"They wouldn't be pointing at you if you were honest." Bill stepped forward and threw his hands up into the air. "Use your brain, Bobby." He growled. With his loud voice and tall, broad frame the man could be intimidating.

"You wouldn't like it if I did, Bill." Bobby moved in his direction, his shoulders high and tense. "Because what my brain is telling me, is something that I don't want to believe."

"I don't know what you're talking about. Just go to the police, Bobby. I can't have this kind of scandal tainting my farm. The police need all the information to solve this." Bill turned and headed for the house.

Bobby stood perfectly still as he stared after him. A flutter of the wind caused the unbuttoned shirt he wore over his t-shirt, to flap at his sides. He slid his hands into the pockets of his well-worn jeans, and his shoulders sank.

Ally stepped out of the car. "Bobby." She

lingered by the car, uncertain if he would be welcoming. He turned to face her.

"Ally." Bobby stared back at her, his expression indifferent and his tone cool. "What can I help you with?"

"I came to see you." Ally took a few steps towards him.

"Why?" Bobby grabbed a bag of seed from a pile beside the barn door and hauled it up onto his shoulder.

"I can't stop thinking about Elisa, and what happened. I know you worked with her. I thought maybe you could help me understand a few things." Ally watched his muscles flex beneath the weight of the heavy bag. When he wasn't joking or laughing, he could be quite an intimidating figure. Although shorter than Bill, he was large, and muscular, and at the moment quite angry.

"What is it that you want to know?" Bobby tossed the bag of seed onto a nearby cart, then shot a look in her direction.

"It just seems to me that you and Elisa must have spent a lot of time working together. You had to have gotten pretty close." Ally took a step out of the way as he hauled another bag up onto his shoulder.

"We were close, I guess. But like I said before she was a private person. I'm still not sure what you're implying." Bobby tossed the bag, with a subtle grunt under his breath.

"Only that you probably knew her the best of anyone else around here. She befriended you, didn't she?" Ally held her breath as she anticipated his reaction to the question. Would he sense that she suspected him and get defensive?

"We were friends." Bobby cleared his throat and turned to face her. This time his entire focus was on her.

"Or more?" Ally dug her heels into the ground as her heart skipped a beat. Would the fury in his eyes spill out into his actions?

"What are you saying?" Bobby crossed the distance between them, his voice a hiss.

"Nothing." Ally held up her hands as her breath caught in her throat. "Bobby, just calm down."

"Nothing?" Bobby's eyes widened. "But you shy back like I'm about to murder you?"

"Bobby, I know that there was something between you two." Ally's stomach twisted as she edged a few steps back. "That's all I know."

"It's kind of a relief." Bobby wiped his hand

across his forehead and closed his eyes. "Only Bill and Starla knew."

"Is that what Bill wanted you to tell the police?" Ally took a step towards him. "That you two were together?"

"We weren't together." Bobby shook his head. "We just sang together."

"You really weren't together?" Ally locked her eyes to his. "I heard that you tried to give her flowers at one of her gigs, but she rejected you."

"Really? I did try to give her flowers, but she didn't reject me. They were a thank you for agreeing to sing with me. She told me to take them home and bring them to work the next day. She didn't want the band members to see me give them to her." Bobby shrugged. He fumbled in his pocket and pulled out a paper bag. He pulled out a cherry from the bag and popped it in his mouth then spat the pit out. Ally frowned as she watched him. "Don't worry, they degrade in the soil. It's a good fertilizer. Do you want one?" He held out the bag.

"No, thanks." Ally stepped back. As he popped another one in his mouth, she recalled the cherry pits at the base of the tree. She had no way to know if Bobby had eaten them, but this certainly made it look like he had. Was he stalking Elisa?

"I wanted her to start a band with me." Bobby closed his eyes. "She was the most amazingly talented musician. She was so smart, but willing to get her hands dirty. When I asked her to sing with me and start a band with me, she agreed. She didn't laugh in my face."

"She was really going to leave Axel's band and start a band with you?" Ally raised an eyebrow.

"She said she would. I never thought she would agree. I have no experience. I just like singing." Bobby shrugged.

"That must have been very special." Ally's heart fluttered. Bobby said he admired her. But was he actually obsessed? Had he been behind that tree watching her? Did she eventually reject him?

"It was. Every moment with her was. She asked me to stop going to her gigs because she was going to tell them she was leaving, and she didn't want any problems between the band members and me." Bobby sighed. "Bill thinks I should tell the police everything, but I think it would just make them suspect me. I didn't hurt her, Ally. I could never do that."

"Even if she chose Axel and his band over you?" Ally tightened her shoulders and looked into his eyes.

"She wasn't going to." Bobby gritted his teeth, then sighed. "But no, even if she had rejected me, I couldn't have hurt her. She was a talented, beautiful person." He threw another cherry pit on the ground. "I would have done anything to protect her, Ally. I never would have hurt her."

"What is this then?" Ally held up the picture Axel had given her. "You certainly look close. Don't you?"

Bobby took the picture from her as his eyes widened.

"Yes, we do, but it's because we are singing together." Bobby smiled slightly. "We were writing a song together, but we never finished it. We never had the chance to." He lowered his eyes. "Where did you get this?"

"I found it." Ally shrugged.

"Okay." Bobby looked skeptical. "I better get going."

Ally watched Bobby push the cart away. Although, she'd come to the farm for answers, she left with even more questions.

CHAPTER 14

*W*hen Ally arrived at the shop, she patted Cinnamon on the way inside. As she stepped inside, her mind was still a muddle of questions. Bobby seemed so genuine in his admiration for Elisa, but that didn't mean that he was innocent. The grief he displayed could just as easily be regret, or guilt. But poison? A fast-acting lethal poison seemed so risky? She went into the courtyard behind the shop and was greeted by a squeal.

"Arnold!" Ally laughed as the pig trotted up to her. "You're looking pretty good there, fellow." She crouched down to stroke the top of his head.

"Clean bill of health." Charlotte smiled as she

crossed her arms and stared at the two. "He gave us quite a scare, though."

"Yes, he did. You hungry little piggy." Ally grinned and gave his back a pat. "I'm glad he's doing well."

"Me too. I have the samples set out, and we are due for a visit from Mrs. Bing, Mrs. White and Mrs. Cale any moment now." Charlotte leaned back against the counter. "So, tell me quick how it went at the farm."

"I'm not sure, Mee-Maw. I went there thinking that Bobby absolutely had something to do with it. But after I spoke to him, something changed. I can't exactly explain it. But I don't see him as a killer. He claims that they were singing together, they were going to start a band together. Apparently, that's why she was leaving Axel's band." Ally frowned as she stepped behind the counter and stowed her purse. "I think he cared about her. I don't think he killed her. I can't be certain that I'm right about it. I know that I need to keep an open mind. Axel on the other hand, he makes me very uneasy."

"I can see why he would." Charlotte adjusted one of the sample trays on the counter.

"What do you mean?" Ally turned to look at her as she headed in the direction of the register.

"I just mean Axel isn't your type of guy. He's rough around the edges. He's abrasive, and wounded. He's a musician." Charlotte chuckled. "Sometimes that's the best description."

"I like musicians." Ally popped open the drawer of the register and checked over the contents. As the bills flipped across her fingertips she wondered if her grandmother had a point. Was she judging Axel just because he was who he was?

"Not musicians like Axel. Look at Luke, he's this solid, good guy. He would never do a thing to hurt you. My best guess is that Axel has a temper, and we've already seen that he was willing to fight with Elisa over their songs. He puts his needs first. There's nothing wrong with your taste, Ally, you've found a wonderful man in Luke, but not every man will be like him." She walked towards the front door to turn the closed sign to open.

"I see what you're saying." Ally sighed as she realized that she had to consider that she might be biased when it came to Axel. "But it's not as if he didn't have motive and opportunity. We know that he was at the farm. We know that he saw Elisa and Bobby together. We know that he was angry about Elisa claiming the songs he wrote were hers. The list of reasons why he might want to kill her, go on and on. He even told me, he didn't care that much for her, it was just fun."

"We may know all of those things, but there is one other thing we know that counts against it." Charlotte turned back to face her. "Axel needed her. His band needed her. In order to continue to be successful, he needed her to be alive. Killing her could have been an act of rage on his part, but poisoning takes premeditation. It takes a well thought out plan, and that isn't usually the result of rage." She adjusted a few of the wooden toys on the shelves near the counter.

"Good point." Ally gazed out through the front windows of the shop, though her focus turned inward, as she reviewed the potential suspects in her mind. "So, we could assume that we are looking for someone who had a calculated reason to want to get rid of Elisa. Not someone who had an angry outburst."

"Yes, I think that's a fair assumption. Her neighbor, Vick, could potentially have been so infuriated by her drumming that he planned something this wicked. However, he is the only one that we can't place at the farm." Charlotte turned on the coffee pots that Ally had prepared. Immediately, the strong aromas of vanilla and cinnamon assaulted her senses.

"Maybe, but that doesn't mean he wasn't there. I mean, what better way to direct attention away from himself than to kill her at the farm?" Ally put a finger to her lips and tipped her head towards the front door just as it swung open. Starla stepped inside with a large box in her hands.

"Morning ladies." Starla smiled at both of them as she carried the box to the front counter. "I bring you gifts."

"Gifts?" Ally smiled in return, then peered over the edge of the box. "What is it?"

"I know there is a lot going on right now, and I just wanted to make sure you had some more fruit. I'd like you to try to make these chocolates a success, and with so much distraction going on I know it will be easy to let it fall to the wayside. Anyway, I hope this will help prevent that." Starla looked between the two with a warm smile. "Plus, it gives me something to do, to keep my mind off things."

"Thank you so much, Starla, that is so kind of you." Charlotte stretched out her hand to her and gave Starla's hand a subtle squeeze as she took it.

"How are you holding up? I can't imagine how upset you must be."

"I try not to let it get to me too much. Yes, it is a tragedy, and it's disheartening to think that something so terrible could happen on my farm. But dwelling on it won't do anyone any good and giving in to my grief will only prevent me from moving forward. So!" Starla took a deep breath and laughed. "I'm focusing only on the positive. As much as I can."

"That seems like a good plan." Ally smiled to herself as she recalled how much better she felt when she kept things upbeat. "You're very wise, Starla."

"Life experience." Starla winked. "So, is this gift enough of a bribe to get some candies made?"

"It certainly is." Charlotte picked up the box. "I'll take it in the back and get things started."

"Great. Let me know when they are ready, and I'll swing by to pick some up. I'd love to try them." Starla blew Charlotte a light kiss from the palm of her hand.

"Will do." Charlotte carried the box to the back. She had no intention of using the fruit from Bill and Starla's farm until she knew it had all been cleared of poison, but she didn't want to offend Starla. She still wanted to discuss a potential business deal with her, but she wanted things to calm down first.

"Thanks again, Starla." Ally smiled as she turned back towards Starla.

"What were you and Bobby talking about today?" Starla locked her eyes to Ally's and the subtle glow of warmth that made them so friendly a moment before, vanished, replaced by a stern expression.

"Oh uh, I didn't know that you saw us." Ally took a slight step back. "We were just discussing Elisa, and his relationship with her."

"I wasn't aware that you were involved in the investigation." Starla's icy tone was in strong opposition to the airy attitude she projected just moments before.

"I'm not." Ally stared back at the woman, her eyes narrowed. She'd never seen this side of Starla before, and she couldn't help but wonder where it was coming from. "I just want to find out what happened to Elisa and make sure Bobby is okay."

"Perhaps you could just let the police do their job." Starla tilted her head to the side, which made her tight smile appear even more tense. "And you could focus on making delicious candy."

"Sure, I guess." Ally's heart pounded as she

thought about the way that Bill had spoken to Bobby earlier in the day. What had crawled so deep under his skin that he felt the need to threaten and intimidate? Why was Starla acting like this? "I'm sorry if you think I'm being callous, Starla. I'm sure that Elisa meant a lot to you."

"Like I said, I didn't know her well." Starla pursed her lips. "Perhaps I should have made more of an effort. Obviously, she had quite a past if she ended up this way."

"You think it may have been someone from her past that killed her?" Ally studied the woman's face. "Did she mention anyone that she might have had problems with?"

"No. I just assumed she left trouble behind. A woman doesn't just reinvent herself for no reason." Starla turned towards the door as it swung open.

Mrs. White, Mrs. Cale, and Mrs. Bing filed in.

"Oh Starla!" Mrs. Bing gasped as she pressed her hand against her chest. "I'm so glad to see you out and about. We've all been terribly worried about you."

"Worried about me?" Starla smiled. "There's no need, but thank you for your concern. I was just on my way out. It was good to see all of you." She waved to the three women, then passed a glance over her shoulder in Ally's direction. "You as well, Ally."

Ally tried to muster up a response, but all she could do was nod. She had no idea how to take Starla's visit, but she was certain it wasn't just about dropping off some fruit.

CHAPTER 15

*M*rs. Bing, Mrs. Cale and Mrs. White buzzed with excitement as they dined on chocolates and enjoyed fresh hot coffee. As they chatted, Ally did her best to put her conversation with Starla out of her mind. Whatever she was up to, it was a distraction. She wanted to figure out if her suspicion of Axel was warranted, and if there might be something more to learn about Vick. Her grandmother was right, he had the time to stew and think about a plan to kill her.

"Mrs. Bing, you mentioned that you spoke to Elisa a few times." Ally interrupted their lively debate about nuts in candy.

"Why yes, not much, though. She seemed like a lovely girl. Why?" Mrs. Bing met her eyes.

"Did it seem as if she had a troubled past? As if she was on the run?" Ally noticed the other two women leaned closer.

"Not at all. She seemed bright, cheerful even. She said she used to work as an accountant. She had only recently graduated, and she worked for just a few months. She got into accounting because of her parents, but she didn't enjoy her old job and now she was doing what she wanted to do. She said that she liked to wander, but Geraltin might be a place she could settle down." Mrs. Bing shrugged. "She reminded me of you, actually."

"Me?" Ally raised an eyebrow.

"Sure. Smart, creative, and so sweet." Mrs. Bing patted Ally's cheek. "You are one of a kind, however."

"Thank you, Mrs. Bing." Ally smiled.

"I used to talk to her in the back, sometimes." Mrs. Bing nodded. "But it was so noisy."

"The back?" Ally asked.

"Yes, at Sally's." Mrs. Bing smiled.

"Sally's?" Ally's mind swirled as the name rang a bell.

"Yes, Sally's bar. It's a bar in Geraltin where they played most of their gigs. I would catch her by

her locker before, or after the set. Usually before."
Mrs. Bing nodded proudly.

"I told you she's a stalker." Mrs. White laughed
as she gestured to Mrs. Bing.

"I am not." Mrs. Bing sighed.

"Did you ever see her with any paperwork?"
Ally asked.

"No." Mrs. Bing shook her head. "Why?"

"Oh, nothing really." Ally sighed. "Her
bandmates said that she had paperwork with her the
night before she was murdered."

"I have never seen her with any." Mrs. Bing
shook her head thoughtfully.

"Do you recognize this?" Ally took the slip of
paper that had stuck to Arnold's hoof out of her purse
and showed it to Mrs. Bing. Her grandmother had
given it to her to see if she could work out what it was.

Mrs. Bing looked at it as she turned the plastic
over in her hand.

"Yes, it's from Sally's." Mrs. Bing nodded. "It
looks like it's been torn off one of their menus."

"Do you know what the number would be for?"
Ally asked.

"No, maybe it's a PIN?" Mrs. Bing frowned.

"Maybe." Ally nodded thoughtfully. She felt as if

she was getting closer, but she couldn't quite fit the pieces together.

"I'll think about it and let you know." Mrs. Bing smiled with determination.

"Thank you." Ally handed each of them a small box of chocolates before they headed out the door, along with the promise of more waiting for them the next day. She was about to head into the kitchen, when the door swung open again.

"Back for more, Mrs. Bing?" Ally flashed a smile in the direction of the door. The smile faded as Detective Pauler came into view.

"Ally." Detective Pauler nodded to her. "I need to speak with you."

"I do as well." Ally rounded the counter. "Did you find out anything about Vick? Elisa's disgruntled neighbor? About his background? Have you spoken to him?"

"Slow down!" Detective Pauler frowned. "I hope you know that I am taking extra time out of my day to meet with you." He smoothed back his hair. "I mean, after our first encounter I didn't really think I'd need to speak to you again. But I know that you have something of interest to me."

"I do?" Ally's eyes widened as she stared at him. "What could I have that's of interest to you?"

"You were around for the final moments of Elisa's life." Detective Pauler stared into her eyes. "Somewhere in that brain of yours, there's a clue locked away, a clue that will tell me exactly who her killer is."

"I wish there was." Ally's heart fluttered at the thought. "If I knew who killed Elisa, I would tell you. I want to find her killer as much as you do, if not more."

"As much as I do? I'm the detective working the case. Why would you think that you want to find her killer more?" The detective's eyes narrowed as if he intended to pick apart every word that came out of her mouth. For an instant she wondered if he was actually looking for a clue that would lead him to the killer, or deciding whether she should be a suspect.

"What about the cherry pits? Hmm? I think that would tell you exactly who the killer was. Someone was watching her. Someone took the time to stake out the shed." Ally took a slight step back behind the counter.

"We don't think we'll be able to get anything off them, but we are trying. The results aren't back, yet. Sorry, it's not like television, where you find one piece of evidence and the crime is solved." Detective

Pauler raised his eyebrows as he set his hands down on the counter. "But I suppose you know that, don't you? Dating a detective?"

"I suppose I do." Ally took a deep breath and reminded herself that making an enemy out of the detective investigating the murder was not a good idea.

"Can you please tell me what I need to know." Detective Pauler gazed into her eyes again.

"I don't know what you want me to tell you. I didn't see or hear anything that day that would implicate any particular person." Ally shrugged. "I wish I could help you, but there is nothing in my head that will solve this crime."

"I think there is. You saw it." Detective Pauler squinted as he studied her. "You saw the murder weapon. It was in that shed with you, and Elisa. As far as we know she never left that shed. Which means that whatever she had, was there when you were there. You saw it, Ally."

"I never thought about that." Ally's eyes widened with the realization. "Maybe you're right, maybe I did see it. But it could have been anything."

"No, it couldn't have." The detective lowered his voice, which drew her closer to the counter again. "It had to be something that only she had. If we can figure out what it was, that should point us in the direction of the killer."

"I have no idea." Ally frowned as she tried to recall the crime scene. There were so many things inside the shed. "Even if I could remember, there's no way that I could be sure."

"Think!" The detective smacked both his hands on the counter with a sudden and sharp strike.

The sound made Ally jump. As her hands flew up in the air in a defensive manner, she recalled grabbing on to the side of the cart to keep herself steady as Bobby drove towards the shed like a madman. Something about that moment drew her attention. Was it his laughter? Was it something in the scenery that they passed by? She recalled every detail she could of the moment that he stopped in front of the shed. Could it have been something on the outside of the shed? Something on the ground? Something that she had in her hands?

"Oh no!" Ally's mind spun and the shop around her grew dim as an awful realization flooded through her.

"What is it?" Detective Pauler's hand jutted out across the counter and caught her elbow before she could tumble backwards. "You remembered something, what is it?"

"No, it can't be." Ally closed her eyes tight.

"Tell me now, Ally. Tell me whatever it is that you remembered. You told me you want to find her killer as much as I do, or even more. Tell me."

As Ally's eyes slowly opened, she found his hard gaze locked to hers.

"It was me," Ally whispered. "I'm the one that killed her."

"What did you just say to me?"

"I mean, I didn't kill her. But I gave her what killed her." Ally looked into his eyes as guilt surged through her. "A bottle of water. I didn't see her drink it, but it could be that, couldn't it?"

"You said you gave it to her? It could be the water, she would have had to have it shortly after you left. But that matches the timeline." Detective Pauler frowned. "I've got to go." He turned away from the counter and started towards the door.

"Detective Pauler, wait!" Ally rounded the counter as she walked after him. "It was Bobby that gave me the water bottle to give to her. I think he might have been the one that left the cherry pits by the tree. He had taught her his family recipes for making the jams. He was also trying to start a band with her, and they sang and wrote songs together. I think there might be a lot more to their relationship."

"Wait, what?" Detective Pauler spun on his heel to face her. "You're just telling me all of this now?"

"Well I—" she paused as she realized there wasn't a good explanation for withholding the information and there was no reason to antagonize the detective by pointing out that she had tried to give him information before and he had all but dismissed it. "Just because they sang together doesn't mean he killed her."

"Let's see. He gave her his recipes for making jams, she then stole the business from him. They sang together. He stalked her. He gave her a poisoned bottle of water. I'd say all of that adds up pretty quickly." Detective Pauler's jaw rippled as he seemed to hold back a few more words. After a sharp breath, he looked at her again. "The next time you get some new information, I should be the first one that you call." Detective Pauler turned on his heel and stalked out of the shop. Ally was stunned that he could blame her when he had been less than welcoming when she had seen him at the police station.

"Ally?" Charlotte stepped out from the kitchen. "Was that Detective Pauler?"

"Yes." Ally frowned as she grabbed a cloth to wipe down the counter. "Yes, it was."

"Why was he talking to you like that?" Charlotte watched her with mounting concern as Ally scrubbed at the counter. "Ally, it's already clean. What's wrong?"

"Oh Mee-Maw, I think that we figured out how Elisa was killed, and I feel just terrible about it." Ally tossed down the cloth on the counter. "I think it was the bottle of water that I gave her."

"Oh Ally, oh no." Charlotte wrapped her arms around her. "Listen sweetheart, even if it was, it's not your fault. It could have just as easily been me that handed it to her. You did nothing wrong."

"I know, I really do know that, but it doesn't stop me from feeling terrible." Ally pulled away from her grandmother and shook her head. "I can't let this be. I have to find out what really happened to Elisa. I know that Detective Pauler is on his way to arrest Bobby, and I know that it's my fault."

"Maybe Bobby really is guilty, Ally." Charlotte grabbed Ally's hands and gave them a firm squeeze. "Take a breath, and think about what you are doing. You can't take all of this on yourself. It's not your responsibility."

"I can't not. I'm sorry." Ally gazed into her eyes.

"Elisa's bandmates told me about some paperwork that she brought home with her, something she was upset about. Maybe it's still at her house."

"I'm sure the police have searched it from top to bottom." Charlotte frowned.

"Maybe, but maybe they overlooked something. I won't know for sure unless I look." Ally glanced up at the clock on the wall. "It won't take me long, maybe an hour, maybe two."

"Ally, I don't care how long it takes you, I'm just not sure it's a good idea. Why don't we close down the shop, and I'll go with you?" Charlotte released Ally's hands and began to pace. "I can be a lookout."

"No Mee-Maw, if we close the shop everyone will know something is up. I promise I'll be careful, in and out in a flash."

"Keep your phone on." Charlotte grasped her shoulders and looked into her eyes. "If there's even a shadow of a problem, get out of there right away."

"I will." Ally gave her a quick hug. "Thanks, Mee-Maw. Even if I don't find anything it will be worth trying."

During the drive to Elisa's house, Ally ran over in her mind everything the detective told her. Was she wrong to think that Bobby wasn't involved? All of the evidence did point in his direction. She parked down the street from Elisa's house, then walked towards it. She knew it was considered part of the investigation, though no crime scene tape was wrapped around it anymore. There were many dark and empty windows to gaze back at her.

Ally took a deep breath as she realized she had no choice. If she wanted to know more about Elisa, then she needed to learn it from the source, and the only way she could do that was by getting inside of the place Elisa considered her home. After a quick glance around to be sure that no one had spotted her, she walked up to the front door. Could it be as easy as opening it? When she tried to turn the knob, it didn't budge. Of course, it was locked. Why wouldn't it be locked? She hurried around the back of the house and tossed a few glances over her shoulder towards the street. So far she hadn't seen another soul. Hopefully, no one had seen her either. At the back door she turned the knob slowly, then with a bit more pressure.

Ally expected to be met with the same resistance as the locked front door. Instead, the knob continued to turn, and she heard the latch give way. Her stomach flipped as she realized that now she had to make a decision. If she stepped through the door she would officially be breaking and entering.

If she stayed outside, she might never find the truth about what Elisa was involved in. Before she could decide whether to push the door open, a sound made her stop in her tracks.

Ally's breath caught in her chest as she heard footsteps behind her. She froze at the sound.

CHAPTER 16

*A*lly turned to find Vick's broad frame in front of her. He pointed a finger at her.

"What are you doing? You aren't allowed in there!"

"What do you mean. I was just walking past." Ally edged back as she watched him. "There's no harm in walking down the street."

"I've already called the police, if you don't want to answer me that's fine, but you're going to answer them." Vick stood in her path.

Ally's heart sank at the idea of the police arriving. Sirens, not far off, made her skin crawl.

"I'm not doing anything wrong." Ally kept her hands in the air. He could still be the one who killed Elisa, and she didn't want to give him any reason to do harm to her. However, the way he stared at her with such determination indicated that he might get more satisfaction from seeing her handcuffed than from seeing her dead.

"Breaking and entering is wrong, young lady. You just stay right where you are."

Ally held her breath as she wondered what he might do if she didn't stay. She could make a run for her car, escape before the police arrived, if he didn't catch her. Then it would be her word against his, wouldn't it? He still couldn't prove that she had tried to enter the house, could he? Flashing lights approached. She bit into her bottom lip. She would be arrested for trying to break in. For trying to enter a crime scene. She would be processed and put into a holding cell. She would be in more trouble than Elisa's killer might ever be.

"I don't know what you're talking about. I was just curious. I just wanted to walk past her house to see if I could get an idea of who might have killed her. Don't you want to have your name cleared?" Ally met his eyes. "Don't you want the police to stop suspecting you?"

"Don't you try to turn this around on me. I have nothing to worry about. I did nothing wrong." Vick glared at her as he took a step closer. "I don't know what you think you might know, but you don't know anything at all. The only person in danger here, is you!"

Before she could say a word, she heard the police cars pull up and their doors push open. Several officers walked towards her.

"Please, this is just a misunderstanding." Ally's heart pounded. She knew it wasn't a misunderstanding. She had tried to enter the house uninvited. If she wasn't caught, she probably would have.

"Ally?" One of the officers stared straight into her eyes. She recognized him as Stuart Caldwell, a friend of Luke's. Part of her was relieved to see him, but another part was mortified. Of course, it wouldn't take long for Luke to find out about this mess, but now she knew he would find out sooner.

"Hi Stuart." Ally frowned as she did her best to hold back her panic. "If you give me a chance, I can clear this all up."

"Spin some lies is what she means." Vick rolled his eyes. "I saw her try to enter the house, where she doesn't belong."

"Why don't we talk over here?" Stuart gestured to the side of the garden.

"I want to see her arrested!" Vick demanded.

"We can't let these crimes go unpunished!"

"What's going on here, Ally?" Stuart looked from Vick to Ally.

Ally turned to face him in time to see him tuck his phone back into his pocket. She had no doubt that he'd just texted Luke.

"Stuart, I didn't do anything. I was just looking at the outside of the house. I just wanted to see if anything popped out at me that might help work out what happened to Elisa." Ally brushed her brown hair back over her shoulders, then glanced down at her wrists, how long would they be free of handcuffs?

"So, you didn't enter the house?" Stuart glanced up as another car pulled into the driveway.

Ally's stomach twisted as she recognized the vehicle. How had Luke gotten there so fast?

"No." Ally looked back at Stuart and lowered her eyes. "No, I was outside the house."

"Ally." Stuart ran his hand across his forehead. "That guy over there, Vick, he's on a first name basis with most of the police officers in Geraltin. He was the wrong person for you to cross."

"What is going on here?" Luke slung his arm around Ally's shoulders and pulled her a few inches back from Stuart.

"What's going on here is that according to the neighbor, Ally tried to break into this house." Stuart pointed at Elisa's empty house, then turned his attention back to Luke. "I'm sorry, Luke, but I have a witness."

As they discussed the situation, Ally wished that she could sink right into the ground. Luke glanced in her direction several times and each time his expression grew darker.

"Look, this must be a mix-up. He probably saw her walking around the house. This was just some kind of mistake. Ally probably thought it wouldn't be a big deal to walk around the outside of the house. I mean technically it's a vacant home at the moment. The owner is deceased, and no other renters have moved in. Did you find any damage to the doors? Any evidence to substantiate his claims." Luke crossed his arms as he stared hard at Stuart.

"Well no, the back door was unlocked when we arrived. The lock wasn't damaged. It wasn't open."

"At the moment, it's the neighbor's word against hers, and it doesn't look like there is any evidence to substantiate his claims." Luke looked over his shoulder at Ally. "No broken locks, nothing stolen."

Ally took a sharp breath and held it.

"I'm sure she didn't enter the property or steal

CINDY BELL

anything." Stuart rolled his eyes. "But I'm the one who has to answer to Detective Pauler about this. What am I supposed to tell him?"

"You could start with the truth." Detective Pauler stepped onto the driveway, his eyes narrowed and his voice firm. "That is always where you should start with me, Officer."

"I'm sorry, sir." Stuart began to explain. When he finished Detective Pauler held up his hand.

"I did not come here for Ally and I'm not concerned with Ally at this time. From what you've told me there is no real evidence of an attempted break-in, so it is her word against his," Detective Pauler said. "Ally can go."

"Yes, sir." Stuart nodded.

"Right now, I want you to arrest Vick." The detective pointed to Vick. Ally's heart jumped into her throat. She couldn't let Vick get into trouble for this. "Make it quick, and don't allow him to make a spectacle." Detective Pauler glanced at his watch. "I want him back at the station right away."

"Arrest Vick?" Stuart's eyes widened. "For this."

Ally was about to tell the detective the whole story so Vick wouldn't get into trouble.

"No, for murder. It's all been approved." The detective waved his hand in the direction of Vick.

"Best to do it now, before he catches wind of what is happening."

"Okay." Stuart nodded, shot one more confused look in his direction, then headed towards Vick.

"Why are you arresting Vick?" Ally stepped in front of the detective before he could walk away.

"Because it turns out Vick has access to the poison through his work. He works at a metal-plating company. He has had some contact with cyanide, which has been identified as the poison that killed Elisa."

"Cyanide! Did the results come back? Was it in the water bottle?" Ally clenched her teeth as she prepared for the answer.

"We never found a water bottle. I know you said you gave her one, but when I checked the evidence collected at the scene, there were no water bottles." Detective Pauler shrugged. "It must not have been in the shed. Right now, I'm not too concerned about it. Hopefully, I can get a confession out of Vick. As for this." He gestured towards the house. "I can't prove anything. But Ally, you really have to stop interfering."

"You're right, I'm sorry." Ally expected to feel relieved that the murder had been solved, but instead she felt more uneasy than ever.

CHAPTER 17

$\mathcal{A}$lly watched Luke drive away. He said everything was fine, and she wanted to trust that, but she knew it must bother him that she had been caught at Elisa's house. Ally's heart continued to race as she drove back to the shop.

When Ally arrived at the shop, she was relieved to see that it was empty. There wouldn't be any nosy questions about what she was up to, or why so many police officers had rushed to Elisa's house. However, as she stepped inside, her grandmother's gaze locked on her, paired with a tight smile.

"How did it go?"

"I almost got busted." Ally sighed as she set her purse down on the counter. "Vick caught me trying to get into the house. Luckily, I hadn't made it

inside, yet. The police showed up, even Luke came."
She shook her head. "At least, they didn't catch me
in there."

"Lucky escape." Charlotte smiled. "I warned
you."

"I know you did. But the good news is that
Detective Pauler arrested Vick. The bad news is,
I'm not convinced that he's the killer." Ally looked
up as the bell over the door jingled. Mrs. Bing
walked in with a huge smile on her face.

"Ladies!"

"Mrs. Bing." Ally smiled. "You look very
happy."

"Well, I am." Mrs. Bing pulled an envelope out
of her purse and put it on the counter. "Look what I
managed to get for you." She looked into Ally's eyes.

"What is it?" Ally looked at the envelope.

"It's from Elisa's locker." Mrs. Bing tapped the
envelope.

"Really?" Ally's eyes widened.

"Yes, I thought that number on the paper you
showed me might be the code to Elisa's locker at
Sally's." Mrs. Bing smiled smugly. "And of course, I
was right."

"You did?" Ally smiled. "Why didn't you say
something?"

"Because I didn't know if it would lead anywhere and I knew that if I told you my suspicions, you would try to access the locker. You would leave me out of it because you would want to protect me." Mrs. Bing plucked a chocolate from the sample tray. "I want a little fun now and then, too."

"How did you manage to get access to the locker?" Ally poured Mrs. Bing a cup of coffee.

"Let's just say being a regular at the bar means that I have made friends with the bouncers there." Mrs. Bing shrugged. "They never think I could be up to no good. I'm just a little old lady to them. So, I said I had left something in the back, and they let me in. I used the code and got the envelope."

"Good work, Mrs. Bing." Charlotte smiled.

"Thank you." Mrs. Bing took another sample chocolate. "I should be an undercover agent. What do you think?"

"Absolutely." Ally winked at her.

"I found the envelope shoved in the back of her locker, under a coat." Mrs. Bing pushed the envelope closer towards Ally and Charlotte. "You asked about whether I had seen her with paperwork, so I thought this might be what you were after. I just don't know what it is."

"I'll look through it with you." Charlotte pulled

some papers out of the envelope and began to thumb through them.

"I may not be able to figure out these numbers, but one thing is very clear to me. These are financial records from Bill and Starla's farm. If Elisa kept them, she had a reason." Ally looked through some of the papers. "I don't want to turn them into the police, yet."

"She used to work as an accountant, maybe she was helping Starla with the books." Charlotte continued to look through the papers.

"Whatever these say, it looks as if it must have been something bad enough that she knew she had to keep it and hide it." Mrs. Bing frowned. "Maybe Christian can help. I know he's investigated some financial stories before." She took another chocolate. Ally wondered if at this rate they would have any left. Undercover work certainly seemed to increase Mrs. Bing's appetite.

"And you're not going to turn this over to Detective Pauler because—?" Charlotte met Ally's eyes.

"Because somehow the water bottle wasn't found at the crime scene, even though we both know that it was there. Because I don't know if I can trust him, or everyone at Geraltin PD. I'm just going to see if I can find out anything about the paperwork before I turn it over to him." Ally shook her head. "He seems to be certain that he arrested the right man. And he may have. But I can't shake this feeling that I am missing something. I'm hoping that Christian will be able to help us sort this out. It could be nothing, or it could be something, and if it has to do with Bill and Starla's farm, I don't want to risk our business relationship by turning this information over to the police unless there is good reason."

"I can understand that." Charlotte filled up the chocolate display.

"I'm going to call Christian and see if he will meet me at the cottage tonight to go over the papers with me." Ally put the papers back in the envelope.

"Oh no, I wish I could join you, but I have line dancing class tonight." Mrs. Bing frowned. "I could always miss the class."

"No, don't do that." Ally shook her head. "You love line dancing, and Mrs. Cale and Mrs. White will expect you there. I promise you I will update you on everything in the morning."

"Thank you." Mrs. Bing stood up from her chair. "Make sure you do." She walked towards the door. Her head held high and her shoulders back. She was clearly proud of her accomplishment.

Ally wanted to see if Luke could help, but she knew he was busy on his case and didn't want to bother him or put Mrs. Bing in an awkward position. She took the phone to the back and dialed Christian's number. She knew that even if he didn't know what the paperwork was right off the bat, he would have the resources to dig into it and get to the truth.

"Christian, can you meet me at the cottage, tonight? I have something you might be able to help me with."

"Sure. Is it about Elisa's murder? I heard that Detective Pauler made an arrest today." A note of skepticism entered his voice.

Ally glanced over her shoulder as her grandmother stepped into the kitchen. She began to spread out the papers on the large table.

"It may be, or it may be nothing. I'm not sure yet. I know Detective Pauler made an arrest, but I'm not entirely convinced that he arrested the right person."

"I'll be there by five. All right?"

"Perfect. Thanks Christian." Ally ended the call, then looked over at her grandmother. "Christian is going to come by. He might be able to make some sense out of this."

"Good." Charlotte turned her attention back to the papers spread out across the table and began to put them together in a pile.

Ally spent the rest of the afternoon making chocolates in between customers. By the end of the day there were several stacks of candy ready to go for the next day.

"Mrs. Bing will be pleased." Charlotte smiled as she wiped her hands on a towel.

"Good." Ally grinned. "She's earned it."

On Ally's way back to the cottage, she considered the possibilities. Was Vick really a killer? Was Bobby involved somehow? She pulled into the driveway, and another car pulled in right behind her. Startled, she got out of the car in the same moment that Christian did.

"A little early, I know." Christian cringed. "Sorry, I just couldn't wait to see what you found."

"It's fine." Ally flashed him a smile as she unlocked the front door. After she greeted Arnold and Peaches, she fed them while Christian looked over the information she'd found.

"Yes, I know what this is." Christian rocked back on his heels, then looked up at Ally. "I think you're going to need to get this to the police right away. But you might not like the results."

"What do you mean?" Ally looked from the numbers, back to him, and frowned. "What is it?"

"You said Elisa used to be an accountant, right?" Christian tapped the paper in front of him. "She must have stumbled across an extra set of books for Bill and Starla's farm. This looks like copies of the books. My guess is, she was helping Starla out with some accounting, from the looks of it she was adding the new jam business to the books. But there are two sets of numbers here. One that tells a significantly less successful story of the farm's profits. Bill and Starla must be attempting to dodge taxes and avoid losing some of the subsidies the farm qualifies for. They're reporting a far lower income than they're actually receiving."

"Oh no." Ally sighed and closed her eyes. "I knew they were hiding something. Elisa must have found out about it, that's why she kept these hidden. Maybe she wasn't sure what to do with them. Maybe she was torn between telling the truth and protecting her bosses. Protecting her job."

"I think you might be right about that. Why else would she have hidden the evidence?" Christian shrugged. "She had the opportunity to turn it in, why didn't she?"

"She might not have had the opportunity. Maybe she was going to turn the evidence in the next day."

"But she was killed before she could." Christian's eyes widened.

"Unless." Ally's stomach churned as she began to process the possibilities that formed in her mind. "Unless, she was scared. Maybe she kept it in an attempt to protect herself."

"Scared of what?" Christian stared at her for a moment, then his eyes widened. "You think Bill might have threatened her?"

"I think Bill and Starla might have done more than that. Starla gave Bobby the bottle of water to give to Elisa, at least according to Bobby. Maybe Bill or Starla poisoned it. Bill was out in the fields. He could have retrieved it. Maybe they thought that if the bottle was never found, the police might have presumed she died from natural causes." Ally narrowed her eyes.

"You're moving quickly on this, Ally. Those are a lot of assumptions. We're talking about pillars of the community. A couple who has owned their farm for decades." Christian frowned.

"Yes, and if Elisa had turned in what she discovered, they would likely lose the farm, especially if they had been submitting fraudulent taxes for years." Ally's heart began to pound. "You're right, I've got to get this information to Detective Pauler. I will take it to him first thing in the morning. I want to make sure that I see him log it into evidence with my own eyes."

"This is going to make a great article once the murder is solved." Christian's lips twitched. "Will you keep me updated?"

Ally could sense the excitement within him.

"Yes, I'll go early in the morning tomorrow and send you a text when it's delivered." Ally walked him to the front door. She still had no idea how she would explain to Detective Pauler how she had gotten the paperwork. She certainly didn't want to get Mrs. Bing into any trouble.

"Thanks Ally. This is going to be big news, not just in Geraltin but here in Blue River, too. If Bill and Starla really were involved in Elisa's murder, it's going to shock a lot of people." Christian stepped out through the door. "I'll be waiting for your text."

CHAPTER 18

Exhausted, Ally made her way back into the living room. As soon as she sat down on the couch, Peaches jumped up onto the cushion beside her. Her tiny paws kneaded at Ally's leg as she attempted to get into her lap.

"Oh Peaches, just what I need, some snuggle time." Ally sat back so that the cat could curl up in her lap. She stroked her soft, orange fur. Ally's thoughts churned. Could Bill and Starla really have been involved in Elisa's murder? Could they have orchestrated the whole thing? If they did, was Bobby aware of it? She closed her eyes and felt the vibrations of Peaches' purr carry through her senses. "Maybe. Maybe they could have done it."

The thought of Bill and Starla being murderers

threatened to turn her world upside down. Her childhood memories, her recent interactions with the couple, none of them indicated that they could be killers. And yet, the more Ally thought about it, the more the possibility seemed very real. They had their life's work to protect. Elisa had the knowledge to shred it to pieces. Had she threatened to turn Bill and Starla in? Had she given away the fact that she knew?

"If Bill and Starla did this, they did it out of fear." Ally sighed as she looked down into Peaches' eyes. "They did it out of greed, to protect themselves. They murdered a young woman who had her entire future ahead of her."

Peaches flicked her tail slowly back and forth as she stared back at Ally. It seemed to Ally that Peaches had a way of giving her advice. Especially when it came to people. She was a great judge of character. "Why did you take off out of that barn, Peaches? I know you are curious, and so is Arnold. But the two of you don't usually get into that much trouble. Did you know what Starla was up to?"

Peaches turned her head into Ally's palm and rubbed it. She gave a loud purr and a swish of her tail.

"Yes, you probably did." Ally scratched behind

Peaches' ear. "That would explain a lot of things. I'm sorry that none of us got there in time to save Elisa."

When her cell phone rang, Ally jolted out of her thoughts. She saw Luke's name on the screen and smiled as she answered.

"Busy afternoon? I haven't heard from you."

"Very. I wanted to check on you. How are things?" Luke asked.

"Good." Ally wanted to tell Luke about what she had found, but she needed to sleep on it first and sort everything out in her mind. She would tell him first thing in the morning. If Luke knew Mrs. Bing had gone to the bar, he wouldn't be happy that she had stuck her nose into things. Ally chewed on her bottom lip. Was she really prepared to accuse Bill and Starla of murder?

"Ally, you need to be careful about what you are doing. You shouldn't have been near Elisa's house like that." Luke's voice grew stern. "You could have been in a lot of trouble."

"Well, rest assured I'm not taking any risks tonight. I'm just going to get a good night's sleep. Hopefully, there won't be anyone peeking in my window to keep an eye on me." Ally smiled to herself.

"I can't make any promises." Luke's voice grew warmer.

"At least knock, I'll let you inside." Ally grinned. "Promise?"

"Always." As Ally ended the call, she shook her head. She felt lucky to have Luke in her life. He cared so much. Elisa wasn't so lucky. She'd had no one to look out for her, to keep her safe while she was in Geraltin. Maybe she had expected Starla to be that person, but things hadn't turned out that way. Had Bobby betrayed her, too? Had he known of Bill and Starla's plan? Or maybe Ally was on the wrong track. Maybe Bobby was the one who discovered what Elisa knew. Maybe Elisa confided in him about it, and warned him that she intended to turn Bill and Starla in. Maybe that had been enough reason for Bobby to kill her, to protect his bosses, the farm, and his livelihood. Who was it that had betrayed Elisa?

CHAPTER 19

*A*fter a quick snack, Ally decided to give herself that sleep that her body ached for. As she prepared for bed, she wondered what the next morning would bring. Would Detective Pauler believe her theory about Bill and Starla? Would he still focus on Vick, Axel and Bobby? She climbed into bed with the symphony of Peaches' and Arnold's snoring to ease her into sleep. However, as she attempted to rest, her thoughts continued to spin. Bill and Starla, beloved residents of Geraltin, and also well known in Blue River and the surrounding towns, murderers? She closed her eyes and recalled the attitude Bill had with Bobby, and the way Starla spoke to her in the shop. Did Bill try to get Bobby to tell the police the truth because he wanted to throw the suspicion off himself and Starla? Ally turned her head into her pillow and sighed. As tired as she was, she just couldn't fall asleep.

The cottage grew noisier every second, from the hum of the air conditioner, to the crickets that must have somehow found their way inside. Everything seemed louder than usual. She pushed the pillow up against her ears and gritted her teeth. If only she could fall asleep, the day could end, and a new one could begin. A new one, hopefully with Elisa's murder solved.

As Ally let the pillow fall back against the bed, she heard a new sound. A subtle sliding. Was it Peaches playing with a toy? She turned her head to see the cat curled up only a few inches from her face. A quick peek over the other side of the bed revealed Arnold still in his bed. What was that sound? She wiped at one eye as she thought about it. It was a familiar sound, but one she couldn't quite place. As she listened for it again, she heard a light knock, as if something had been bumped into. Her heart skipped a beat as she realized what the sliding sound was. It was the sound of the back door opening. It sat a little low and swept across the floor, and when it reached the wall it always knocked into the doorstop.

Every muscle in Ally's body tensed as she became distinctly aware that there was someone else in the cottage. Her grandmother would never sneak in during the middle of the night, and neither would Luke. She recalled joking with him about him peeking in the window. Had he decided to take that as an invitation to surprise her? She couldn't imagine him ever thinking that was a good idea. No, it wasn't Luke. As much as she wanted it to be him, she knew deep down that he would never do that. Reluctantly, she sat up in her bed and listened closely. Yes, that was a footstep. It was muffled by the carpet, but it was there. Her stomach twisted. Why would someone be in her house?

It didn't matter why. She had to act fast. As she began to climb out of bed, Peaches stirred. She lifted her head, looked at Ally, tilted her head to the side, then curled back up. When there was a subtle thump, the cat suddenly bolted upright on all four legs. She looked towards the door, her ears flattened, and her tail rigid.

"Shh." Ally gave Peaches a light pat on the head to calm her.

Arnold continued to snore, but kicked one hoof, as if he might be dreaming.

Ally crept towards the bedroom door. She rarely closed it at night as the animals liked to be able to roam. With every step that brought her closer to the door she knew that she would soon confront the intruder. She had no idea who to expect. Her mind flitted from Bobby, to Axel, even to Detective Pauler. Or Bill and Starla? Was it one intruder or two? Her breath caught in her throat. Had they come there to find the financial records? Did they somehow find out that Ally had them? She froze for a few seconds and listened.

In the kitchen, drawers slid open and closed. They barely made a sound, but Ally could hear it.

Ally became aware that she'd left her phone to charge in the kitchen. Usually, she had it in her room, but she'd plugged it into the charger while she prepared her snack and had never gone back to get it. With no way to call for help, she could only look for something to defend herself with. Beside her bedroom door was the hall closet. She had a vacuum, a mop, and an ironing board in there.

As Ally tried to decide which would make the best weapon, she heard rummaging on the coffee table. The intruder had moved into the living room.

Which meant she might be able to get to her phone. But she would have to risk drawing the intruder's attention. Still, if she didn't get to her phone and call for help, then she would not be found, and she had no idea what the intruder's intentions might be. Was there more than one person? Was the person armed? Did she have only moments to live? She held her breath as she edged forward into the kitchen. She was almost to her phone when the hairs on the back of her neck stood up. She froze. She didn't have to turn around to know that she had been spotted. With her heart in her throat, she turned slowly to face the figure that now filled the kitchen doorway.

"Ally, I wish it hadn't come to this."

CHAPTER 20

Starla drew back the hood from her head and stared into Ally's eyes.

"You should never have gotten involved."

"You involved me when you killed Elisa on the day my grandmother and I visited your farm." Ally did her best to sound bold, but her heart slammed against her chest. Only a few feet away, her phone chirped. Was it a text? Was it Luke? She had no idea, and she might never find out.

"I didn't want to kill anyone. It's such dirty business. But that girl." Starla shook her head as she clenched her jaw. "She wouldn't listen to reason. All I did was ask her to add her business to the farm's books. The books I gave her. But when she put the notebook back, she discovered my other records, my real records. I offered to cut her in on the profits and explained how it worked. But she refused. She said it wasn't right, and that she didn't want to have anything to do with it." Starla licked her lips and looked up at the ceiling, then back at Ally. "I was going to let it go at that. She didn't have any proof to make any accusations."

"What about Bill?" Ally asked. "Did he help you? Is he here?"

"No, of course not. He had no idea what was going on. He doesn't care about the figures as long as there is food on the table. He leaves all of the financials to me. He had nothing to do with this. If he knew what I had been doing, he would have been furious. Everything has to be above board. He even got angry with Bobby for not telling the police the whole truth about him and Elisa singing together and forming a new band. He always thought that the truth was better no matter the consequences."

"Well, maybe he's right," Ally offered.

"Sometimes you have to do things that aren't on the straight and narrow to protect the people you love. The things you have worked so hard for." Starla's face hardened with determination. "Elisa threatened to tell Bill. I had to protect my marriage."

All at once the pieces fell together in Ally's mind.

"You did this alone. You gave the water bottle to Bobby to give to Elisa. You tampered with it before you passed it to him. You also had the chance to go back and retrieve the bottle. That's why Peaches and Arnold were able to escape the barn." Ally looked at Starla. "You left them there alone. You knew you had to get the water bottle back before Elisa's body was found, otherwise it would point back to you. If you hopped on a golf cart and drove a different path it would have been tight, but possible for us to miss each other."

"Well done, Ally." Starla slowly clapped her hands together.

"How did you get the poison?" Ally asked.

"Oh, we have had it for years. In the old days we used it with other chemicals to kill pests." Starla shrugged. "I was meant to get rid of it years ago but I thought one day I might need it, and I was right of course. You can never be too prepared." She smiled. "You see I had no choice I had to protect myself, my husband, our farm. That night when I found all of my records missing, I knew that she had taken them. She was the only one who knew about them. But I couldn't confront her about it. I needed to get them back. That following morning, I went to her house after she left for work. I found the paperwork and took it back. She left the books on her desk in plain sight. I knew she might have made copies, but it was a risk I had to take. I thought it would be okay because I acted quickly and got the originals. Once I had the original account books, I had to make a decision." She drew a deep breath. "A terrible decision."

"That wasn't the only decision that you could have made." Ally narrowed her eyes. "You could have done so many other things. You could have told the truth. Instead, you chose to end the life of an innocent person."

"Oh yes, you think you're so much better than me?" Starla chuckled, then scowled. "Tell me that when you've worked your fingers to the bone for decades just to get a little something for yourself. When you watch your husband work every day of his life. Tell me that when you might be faced with spending the last twenty years of your life in prison. You think you'd do something different?"

"I think I wouldn't have been dishonest in the first place," Ally mumbled as she noticed a handle that stuck out of Starla's belt. Was it a knife?

"Looking back now, I wish I had made better choices. But it's impossible to travel back through time, isn't it?" Starla rested her hand on the handle. "Now we need to talk about choices, Ally. We need to figure out how we move on from here."

"Starla, there are ways you can still help yourself. There are still good choices you can make. Just let me call Luke, he can come over, and we can all talk about this together." Ally smiled as she shrugged. "It doesn't have to be as bad as you think."

"It does." Starla frowned. "I'm sorry, Ally, but I can't spend the rest of my life in prison, I can't lose my farm. Just like I couldn't have Elisa knowing the truth, I can't have you knowing the truth. There really is only one choice." She lunged towards Ally in the same moment that she jerked the knife out of her belt.

Ally gasped and dodged out of the way in the direction of her phone. She managed to grab it as she ducked Starla's next swing. She didn't dare to look at the phone as she fumbled with the screen and did her best to put the kitchen table between herself and Starla.

"Stop Starla! You don't have to do this!" Ally dropped the phone as she jumped out of the way of another strike.

"You left me no choice, Ally!"

Suddenly, Ally heard a shriek. It wasn't a shriek from Starla, or from herself, but from a very familiar snout. Arnold charged forward, his head down, as he aimed for Starla.

"Get out of here!" Starla swung one foot towards the pig but Arnold powered forward into her legs. Starla screamed and lost her balance. Ally jumped forward and snatched the knife from Starla's hand just before she hit the floor.

Arnold charged over Starla until he was positioned on her chest. He stuck his nose up to her face and grunted. Peaches climbed on top of Arnold as if she was helping Arnold keep Starla restrained. Ally hadn't even seen the cat slip in.

"Don't move, Starla." Ally warned as she moved closer to the woman. "Don't get up."

"No, this can't be happening!" Starla gasped as tears flooded down her cheeks.

Outside, Ally heard sirens. For the first time she heard a voice shouting through her phone.

"We're here, Ally, we're here!"

Luke's words reached her as she continued to point the knife in Starla's direction. Relief caused her knees to feel weak for a few moments. It was over. Elisa's murderer had been caught, and soon she would be safe.

As the police rushed into the house, Ally reached down to guide Peaches off Arnold and Arnold off Starla. Peaches sidled closer to him and gave his ear a light lick.

"You two make a great team." Ally smiled through tears as she stroked both of them.

Starla submitted to the handcuffs, as if she had no fight left in her.

"Ally!" Luke bolted into the kitchen and took the knife from her hand. He turned it over to an officer, then wrapped Ally up in his arms. "Please tell me you're okay."

"I'm fine." Ally wiped at her eyes, then kissed his cheek. "Thanks to some small heroes, and a great boyfriend who answered my call."

"I almost hung up. I thought it was an accident." Luke shuddered as he held her tighter. "Then I heard Arnold shriek. I knew that wasn't normal. I knew something was wrong."

"I'm so glad you came." Ally buried her face in the curve of his neck and took a deep breath of his cologne. She wanted more than anything to stay in his arms for as long as she could. But she knew the questions would come. As Luke guided her towards the kitchen table, Detective Pauler stepped inside.

He looked from Ally, to Starla, as she was led towards the front door.

"Are you okay, Ally?" Detective Pauler asked.

"I'm fine." Ally nodded, then did her best to smile.

"Elisa got her justice, thanks to you." Detective Pauler shook his head as he ran his hand back through his hair. "Starla wasn't even on my radar."

"You would have figured it out, eventually." Ally shrugged.

"Maybe I need to take some detective lessons from you." Detective Pauler grinned and offered his hand.

"Anytime." Ally smiled as she shook it.

Luke laughed and kissed the top of her head.

"She's the best detective I know."

The End

RASPBERRY WHITE CHOCOLATE CAKE RECIPE

INGREDIENTS:

Cake

2 cups all-purpose flour

1 teaspoon baking powder

1/2 teaspoon baking soda

1/2 cup butter (room temperature)

1 1/4 cups superfine sugar

2 large eggs

1 teaspoon vanilla extract

1 cup buttermilk

White Chocolate Buttercream Frosting

RASPBERRY WHITE CHOCOLATE CAKE RECIPE

10 ounces white chocolate
1 cup butter
1 1/2 cups confectioners' sugar

2 cups raspberries
1/2 cup raspberry jam

PREPARATION:

Preheat the oven to 350 degrees Fahrenheit.

Grease 2 x 8-inch round cake pans.

Sift the flour, baking powder and baking soda into a
bowl.

In another bowl cream the butter and superfine
sugar until light and fluffy. Mix in the eggs and
vanilla extract.

Add the dry ingredients alternating with the
buttermilk to the butter mixture. Mix until
combined.

Divide the mixture between the 2 cake pans.

Bake in the pre-heated oven for 20-30 minutes. The cakes are ready when a skewer inserted into the center comes out clean. Leave aside to cool and then remove from the pans for frosting.

To make the frosting, melt the chocolate and let it cool. Cream the butter and confectioners' sugar. Once combined mix in the melted chocolate.

Take one of the cakes and spread the raspberry jam over the top. Spread a layer of the frosting over the jam. Place the other cake on top.

Frost the top and sides of the cake. Decorate the top of the cake with raspberries.

Enjoy!!

ALSO BY CINDY BELL

CHOCOLATE CENTERED COZY MYSTERIES

The Sweet Smell of Murder

A Deadly Delicious Delivery

A Bitter Sweet Murder

A Treacherous Tasty Trail

Pastry and Peril

Trouble and Treats

Fudge Films and Felonies

Custom-Made Murder

Skydiving, Soufflés and Sabotage

Christmas Chocolates and Crimes

Hot Chocolate and Homicide

Chocolate Caramels and Conmen

Picnics, Pies and Lies

Devils Food Cake and Drama

Cinnamon and a Corspe

DONUT TRUCK COZY MYSTERIES

Deadly Deals and Donuts

Fatal Festive Donuts

Bunny Donuts and a Body

Strawberry Donuts and Scandal

Frosted Donuts and Fatal Falls

NUTS ABOUT NUTS COZY MYSTERIES

A Tough Case to Crack

A Seed of Doubt

Roasted Penuts and Peril

WAGGING TAIL COZY MYSTERIES

Murder at Pawprint Creek

Murder at Pooch Park

Murder at the Pet Boutique

A Merry Murder at St. Bernard Cabins

Murder at the Dog Training Academy

DUNE HOUSE COZY MYSTERIES

Seaside Secrets

Boats and Bad Guys

Treasured History

Hidden Hideaways

Dodgy Dealings

Suspects and Surprises

Ruffled Feathers

A Fishy Discovery

Danger in the Depths

Celebrities and Chaos

Pups, Pilots and Peril

Tides, Trails and Trouble

Racing and Robberies

Athletes and Alibis

Manuscripts and Deadly Motives

Pelicans, Pier and Poison

SAGE GARDENS COZY MYSTERIES

Birthdays Can Be Deadly

Money Can Be Deadly

Trust Can Be Deadly

Ties Can Be Deadly

Rocks Can Be Deadly

Jewelry Can Be Deadly

Numbers Can Be Deadly

Memories Can Be Deadly

Paintings Can Be Deadly

Snow Can Be Deadly

Tea Can Be Deadly

Greed Can Be Deadly

Clutter Can Be Deadly

BEKKI THE BEAUTICIAN COZY MYSTERIES

Hairspray and Homicide

A Dyed Blonde and a Dead Body

Mascara and Murder

Pageant and Poison

Conditioner and a Corpse

Mistletoe, Makeup and Murder

Hairpin, Hair Dryer and Homicide

Blush, a Bride and a Body

Shampoo and a Stiff

Cosmetics, a Cruise and a Killer

Lipstick, a Long Iron and Lifeless

Camping, Concealer and Criminals

Treated and Dyed

A Wrinkle-Free Murder

A MACARON PATISSERIE COZY MYSTERY SERIES

Sifting for Suspects

Recipes and Revenge

Mansions, Macarons and Murder

HEAVENLY HIGHLAND INN COZY MYSTERIES

Murdering the Roses

Dead in the Daisies

Killing the Carnations

Drowning the Daffodils

Suffocating the Sunflowers

Books, Bullets and Blooms

A Deadly Serious Gardening Contest

A Bridal Bouquet and a Body

Digging for Dirt

WENDY THE WEDDING PLANNER COZY MYSTERIES

Matrimony, Money and Murder

Chefs, Ceremonies and Crimes

Knives and Nuptials

Mice, Marriage and Murder

ABOUT THE AUTHOR

Cindy Bell is a USA Today and Wall Street Journal Bestselling Author. She is the author of the cozy mystery series Wagging Tail, Donut Truck, Dune House, Sage Gardens, Chocolate Centered, Macaron Patisserie, Nuts about Nuts, Bekki the Beautician, Heavenly Highland Inn and Wendy the Wedding Planner.

Cindy has always loved reading, but it is only recently that she has discovered her passion for writing romantic cozy mysteries. She loves walking along the beach thinking of the next adventure her characters can embark on.

You can sign up for her newsletter so you are notified of her latest releases at http://www.cindybellbooks.com.